Acclaim for *1*
by Dave Cou

'This heartfelt, well-told debut is a delight.'
Nicolette Jones, *Sunday Times*

'Unputdownable . . . a jewel of a book.'
Candy Gourlay, author of *Tall Story*

'If you're only going to take my advice once this year make it this book.'
Sarah Gibson, FEELING FICTIONAL

'Some books you read and find entertaining. And some books you read and never forget. This is one I will have in my mind for a long time.'
Paula Hardman, PAULASHX

'I want to put this book in every teenager's hand.'
Vivienne Dacosta, SERENDIPITY REVIEWS

'Cousins is a truly powerful writer, managing to have me laughing out loud during one scene and crying during the next . . . a fresh, exciting new voice who isn't afraid to tell it like it is.'
Carly Bennett, WRITING FROM THE TUB

'The ability to make light of the harshest of realities and bring humour into the darkest of circumstances sets Dave Cousins' writing apart. Think Jacqueline Wilson for boys!'
THE BOOK KEEPER

'A wonderful, uplifting book, a fabulous story of friendship, loyalty, ingenuity, and brotherly love.'
BOOKS FOR KEEPS

WAITING FOR GONZO

DAVE COUSINS

OXFORD
UNIVERSITY PRESS

OXFORD
UNIVERSITY PRESS

Great Clarendon Street, Oxford OX2 6DP
Oxford University Press is a department of the University of Oxford.
It furthers the University's objective of excellence in research, scholarship,
and education by publishing worldwide in

Oxford New York

Auckland Cape Town Dar es Salaam Hong Kong Karachi
Kuala Lumpur Madrid Melbourne Mexico City Nairobi
New Delhi Shanghai Taipei Toronto

With offices in

Argentina Austria Brazil Chile Czech Republic France Greece
Guatemala Hungary Italy Japan Poland Portugal Singapore
South Korea Switzerland Thailand Turkey Ukraine Vietnam

First published 2013

British Library Cataloguing in Publication Data

Data available

ISBN: 978-0-19-274546-0
1 3 5 7 9 10 8 6 4 2

Printed in Great Britain
Paper used in the production of this book is a natural,
recyclable product made from wood grown in sustainable forests.
The manufacturing process conforms to the environmental
regulations of the country of origin.

For my grandparents
with love and thanks for sharing their
stories with me.

MESSAGE TO GONZO

Listen, G—this is important and there isn't much time.

I want you to know what really happened, because things weren't supposed to end like this.

I blame Marcel Duchamp, but he's dead, so there's not much anybody can do to him now. When he drew a moustache and a goatee beard on a copy of the *Mona Lisa*—which is probably the most famous painting in the world—he said he did it because he wanted to challenge people's perception of what art could be.

He was lying.

He did it because it was funny.

Moustaches are funny.

End of story.

Except in this case, G—it was just the beginning.

THE BEGINNING

G MINUS 245

ONE

DOING A PETE TAYLOR

Do you know what my loving mother said as she dropped me off outside Crawdale High School? Not, *Have a nice day, darling!* Not even, *Good luck*. No, what she said to me was:

'Now, Marcus, remember—first impressions last—so don't be cocky.'

She's right about one thing though, G—when you start a new school, you have to make the right first impression. Not like Pete Taylor. He arrived at the beginning of Year Five, and in the first hour of his first day, peed himself in class. Pete was funny, clever, and brilliant at sport. But when I left Hardacre four years later, he was still known by everyone as Wee Pete.

Now, don't get me wrong, G, I wasn't worried about losing control of my bladder as I walked into school that morning, but there are more ways than one of doing a Pete Taylor.

'This is Ryan. He'll show you the ropes.' The Head of Year Nine smiled and gestured towards the figure that had appeared in the doorway of his office. The kid seriously needed a haircut. You could barely see his eyes for the mass of brown curls falling over his face.

'Welcome to the school!' Ryan's arm shot out towards me and I realized he wanted to shake hands. 'I'm Ryan.'

'Oz.' We shook and I smiled. See—friendly, not cocky.

'I'm your buddy,' said Ryan. 'To help you settle in. So if there's anything you want to know, just ask.' His accent was so strong I had to concentrate hard to understand what he was saying.

'OK.'

'The school was built in eighteen seventy-five and opened with a class of twenty-three pupils,' he said, as I followed him up a flight of stairs. 'It now has over seven hundred.' Ryan sounded like a museum tour guide, and I wondered if he had been told to give me this information, or if he actually thought I might be interested.

'The school motto is, *libertas a scientia venit,* which is Latin for . . . *from knowledge comes freedom,* or something like that.' He shrugged. 'Is there anything you want to know? Or shall I just keep going?'

'Don't worry. I doubt I'll be staying long,' I said. 'Once my parents wake up from their delusion that moving here was a good idea, we'll be back to civilization—shops and pavements and roads with white lines down the middle!'

Ryan frowned. 'Where is it you're from then?'

'Hardacre—just outside London.'

'So why d'you move here?'

'No choice. My mum got a job at the college up here. Apparently she and Dad always wanted to live in the country. They didn't even ask us!'

'Us?'

'I've got a sister. Not important. The point is we weren't even consulted. It was just—*pack your stuff, we're moving.*'

I shook my head. 'I mean, I bet your mum and dad wouldn't do that to you.'

'They died when I was five,' said Ryan.

'Oh . . . sorry.'

He shrugged. 'I don't really remember them. But I don't think my grandad would do anything like that, not without asking me first.'

'Exactly!' I said. 'And the place they bought—*Scar Hill Farm*! It's like something out of a horror movie—all creaking floorboards and boarded up windows—it's a dump. It even smells like someone died in there . . . ' Too late I realized what I'd said.

I blundered on hoping Ryan hadn't noticed. 'I mean, there's holes in the floor and the roof leaks . . . there's not even any heating.'

We turned into a long corridor. Halfway down, Ryan stopped outside a door marked 9F. 'This is our form room,' he said. 'Registration's at eight-forty and two-fifteen, except Tuesdays and Thursdays, when we have assembly in the main hall.' Then he opened the door and every face in the room swung towards me.

I don't know what I was expecting. Rows of long benches with kids clutching chalk, hunched over slates perhaps. In truth the classroom didn't look all that different to the ones at my old school, but that just made it feel even more alien somehow.

I could sense everyone in the room sizing me up. They'd already been back a couple of weeks. I was something new, a diversion from the mundane. Fresh meat.

'Marcus Osbourne, isn't it?' said the teacher, a round woman in square glasses who introduced herself as Mrs Pike.

'Yeah, but most people call me Oz.'

Someone sniggered at the back of the room and Mrs Pike grimaced. 'I think we'll stick with Marcus, thank you.'

I didn't say anything, but inside my head a voice was protesting, *but . . . I'm* Oz.

'I believe you've just moved into the area, Marcus. Where are you living?'

'Um . . . some place called Slowleigh.'

More snorts of laughter. I guessed some of them had seen the place.

The teacher nodded. '*Slowel*,' she said. 'Round here, we don't always pronounce words how they're spelt, I'm afraid.' Mrs Pike smiled. 'But don't worry, you'll get used to it.'

I wasn't planning on sticking around long enough to get used to anything.

Looking back now, I can see how everything that day was leading up to the moustache, pushing me towards it like arrows painted on the ground. I was just a spoke in the Wheel of Destiny as it rolled towards its inevitable conclusion. What I'm saying, G, is that it wasn't entirely my fault.

My first lesson that morning was Art, which is how I came to find out about Marcel Duchamp and the moustache on the *Mona Lisa*. Had it been English, or French, or History, maybe none of this would have happened.

I found a seat at the back of the room, next to a super-sized kid called Gareth, and watched as everyone began pulling pencil cases and sketchbooks from their bags.

Now you remember how I said there are more ways than one of doing a Pete Taylor? Well . . . opening your rucksack and having your sister's bra fall out onto the table is definitely on the list.

It took me a few seconds to register. I mean, it made no sense for there to be a bra in my bag. But there it was—black and lacy—curled up like a dead bat on my desk.

Unfortunately, this was long enough for Gareth to notice and nudge his mate. Who, by the time I had grabbed the offending article and crammed it back into the bag, had texted every kid in Year Nine, including an internet geek called Mark Edwards. He posted the information to five social networking sites, circulating the news to over thirty countries around the world, all before Mr Henson looked up and asked what was going on.

I opened my mouth, but the words refused to come out, obviously too embarrassed to be associated with me.

'He's got a load of bras in his bag, sir!' said Gareth. There was a noise of grating furniture as everyone in the room turned in our direction.

Meanwhile, my brain was frantically scrolling back to the moment Mum had dropped me off outside school. I saw myself grabbing one of the rucksacks from the pile of bags in the back of the van—bags of washing that Mum was taking to the launderette.

'I must have picked up the wrong bag . . . by mistake.' My cheeks were so hot, I was surprised my hair hadn't ignited.

'That's unfortunate.' The teacher was struggling not to laugh. 'I don't suppose there's anything useful in there? Like a pen or a pencil, perhaps?'

I stared at him, unable to move. It felt like my body had shut down from shame.

'Maybe you'd like to have a look?' suggested Mr Henson.

I nodded and unzipped the rucksack again, even though I knew it was pointless.

Gareth leaned in for a closer look. 'Hey! There's kecks in there an' all! Are they clean?'

I knew I should say something. Something funny and clever. Something Oz would say, but my mind was suddenly blank.

'Perhaps you could lend Marcus a pen for the day, Gareth,' said Mr Henson.

Gareth placed a biro onto the desk with a flourish. 'There you go, Kecks!' he said, and the laughter poured down like hailstones.

It was funny. I knew it was funny. So why didn't I feel like laughing?

I tell you, G—Pete Taylor had nothing on me.

TWO

KECKS

When I got to the next lesson, I had to explain all over again why I didn't have any of the things I needed. Gareth kindly supplied the details I missed out—such as the fact that my bag was full of girls' underwear.

I had to get rid of the rucksack. It was like a beacon of shame hanging off my shoulder.

At break time I found the locker I'd been issued. I was expecting it to be empty, or maybe contain a pair of old trainers or PE socks, but what I saw inside made me stop. In the very centre of the metal box was a pen. One of those fat, smelly markers, standing on end. Now when I say centre, I mean exactly that. I was fairly sure that if I measured the distance from the object to each of the four walls, the numbers would be equal. For some reason it made me think that the pen had been put there on purpose, for me—which was ridiculous, of course. The marker had been left like that as a joke. So slipping it into my pocket made no sense at all. But that's what I did.

Then I stuffed the rucksack into the space and slammed the door.

Just before lunchtime the fire alarm went off. I followed everyone out onto the field, looking for smoke, hoping the school might burn down and the rucksack with it. But of course it was just a drill. By the time we were allowed back inside, the queue for the canteen was longer than it should have been. If the line hadn't been so long, it wouldn't have stretched all the way down the corridor to the noticeboard with all the photographs.

There were loads of them, pictures of school teams and house captains, kids receiving awards and acting in school plays. I wasn't really interested, just trying to avoid eye contact with the group of girls from my art class who were in front of me in the queue.

'Where's your bag at, Kecks?' I pretended I hadn't heard. Then the nearest girl prodded me with a finger. 'Askin' you a question.'

'What?'

'What?' she repeated, doing what she obviously thought was a great impression of my accent. All her mates fell about laughing like it was the funniest thing they'd ever heard. Then they all started up—'What? What? What?'—it sounded like a flock of seagulls.

'Look at his shoes!' said another, pointing.

I looked down at my feet, wondering for a moment if I'd accidentally come to school in Dad's plastic clogs—but I was just wearing my school shoes. Admittedly, they were slightly more pointy than most people's, and had the classic *D-tag* logo embossed on the side. All my mates had a pair back home.

'You never seen a pair of 'tags before?' I asked the girl.

She frowned and looked at her mates. 'What's he say?'

And then she said something else that I couldn't make out and they all laughed.

I didn't realize Gareth was behind me until he spoke. 'Where d'you say you come from again, Kecks?'

'Hardacre—near London.'

'Right, that explains it. Lots of blokes wear women's undercrackers down there do they?' The *What? What? Girls* thought this was hilarious.

'You know, they're actually a lot more comfortable than you'd expect,' I said, smiling at Gareth, even though my heart was playing pinball against my ribs.

He frowned.

'I like a good strong gusset though—for extra support, yeah?'

Gareth blinked, and then he laughed.

'You should try it, honestly,' I said. 'It's all about achieving a balance—comfort and style. You know, the choice of underwear tells you a lot about a person.'

Ryan was in the line behind Gareth, watching me through his hair while his jaw sagged in disbelief. I pointed to the freckle-faced kid standing next to him.

'Now, at a guess I'd say you were a traditional briefs man. Am I right?'

Gareth snorted and the kid blushed.

I noticed other people in the queue were listening now.

'Did you know that you can tell the underwear someone is wearing, purely by looking at their face?'

'Go on then,' said Gareth.

I pretended to think, frowning up at him. 'Skin colour suggests good circulation, so I'd say boxers?'

He laughed. 'See, I knew Kecks were the right name for you!'

The *What? What? Girls* giggled.

I looked around for another target and that's when the photographs on the noticeboard caught my eye. I pointed to a girl holding a trophy and squinting into the camera. 'This one looks in pain,' I said. 'G-string riding high, no question. Might need to send in the retrieval squad for that one!' That got a laugh. 'Briefs, boxers, boxers, commando!' I said, moving along the row of images. Then my eyes rested on the picture of a girl with her arms folded, staring defiantly out of the frame.

'Now *this* is not a happy face,' I said. Which is when the image of the *Mona Lisa* dropped into my head like the next slide in a presentation. 'In fact, this reminds me of someone.'

The corridor shrank back, fading as the image of the girl filled my vision and my fingers started to tingle. I knew what I had to do—what the picture was begging me to do. Then I remembered the marker pen in my pocket and realized I'd been right all along. It *had* been left there for me—for this very purpose. It was like a confirmation: *here is the tool with which to complete your task.*

I knew before I popped the cap that the pen would work. I watched it moving towards the photograph, drawn by a force I was powerless to resist—the Wheel of Destiny rocking on its blocks, anxious to get moving.

'What you doing?' I recognized Ryan's voice, but it sounded distant, like somebody shouting a warning from far away.

All my attention was fixed on the thick black line curling out from beneath the girl's nose. I drew a matching swirl on the other side, taking my time, making sure they were even. Then I filled in the outline with broad vertical strokes, the ink squeaking and glistening on the surface of the paper. For a final flourish I added a pair of glasses—and it was done.

The moment I finished, the clamour of the corridor rushed back in, and Ryan was suddenly at my side.

'You shouldn't have done that,' he whispered, his eyes wide.

'It's just a joke.'

He looked like he was about to say more, but then Gareth put a heavy arm around my shoulders and laughed.

'Now that *is* funny, Kecks,' he said. 'Dead funny.'

THREE

DEAD FRANK

If nowhere has a middle, then this is it. Considering there's nothing here, Slowleigh village is quite easy to find on a map. Head north on the motorway until the thick blue line runs out and keep going, past all the coloured clumps of towns, to the white part of the page, where the roads look like creases on a face, and there it is—a cluster of tiny rectangles on the side of a hill. You can't miss it, because there's nothing else for miles around.

What the map doesn't show is how empty it feels. How, the moment you step outside, the wind tries to hurl you off the hillside. Even when you're indoors you can feel it shaking the house and rattling the windows—hear it trying to pluck the tiles from the roof and sling them into the valley. The squiggles on the page don't show how the landscape stretches, devoid of life in all directions, rolling out beneath an endless lead-bellied sky.

It's not even a proper village, just a scattering of buildings, as though somebody started to construct a town and then died halfway through. Apart from the Beckett Arms pub, the church, and one of those shops that sells everything, but is only open for half-an-hour, twice a week—there's nothing here. I thought the name was a joke until I saw the place. But they got it wrong, G. Life doesn't move slowly here. It's stopped completely. Dead.

The sound of the bus faded, leaving me alone with the wind. I looked around at the bustling heart of my village, silent and empty in both directions. The only sign of life was the pathetic bleating of sheep rolling towards me like tumbleweed. A few metres to my left a ragged ginger cat strolled into view, sat down in the middle of the road, and proceeded to wash its arse.

If we were still living in Hardacre, I would have been walking home with Jack and the others right now, or round at Frog's house playing *SlamShowdown*. I reached inside my blazer for my mobile and was surprised to see I had a signal. I hit Jack's number on speed-dial and felt my heart quicken as the phone rang in my ear.

'Y'ello!'

'Jack!' It came out in a croak.

'Who's that?' I recognized the music from *SlamShowdown* playing in the background, and the clangs and grunts of combat.

'It's Oz!'

'Oz, my man! Hey, it's Oz!' I heard familiar voices behind Jack in the room, and my throat felt tight all of a sudden.

'Hey, man, what's up? How's life on the farm?' said Jack.

'It's crock, man! There's nothing here. Just fields and sheep!'

Jack laughed.

'It's like I've been sent back in time!'

'Use the drop-kick!'

'What?'

'Oooh! Yeah, yeah, yeah!' said Jack. 'Sorry, mate, what were you sayin'? Tuna just got a slam down against *Mighty Martha*! TKO!'

'Yeah? Nice one!' None of us had managed to defeat *Mighty Martha* in *SlamShowdown* before.

'That was the beans, man!' he said, and I could hear them whooping and giving each other high-fives. The line crackled.

'Since when was Tuna any good at *Slam*?'

Jack chuckled. 'He stayed over mine last Friday for some intensive training. He's still crock though. Frog found a cheat on the net.'

I forced a laugh, trying to ignore the jealousy bubbling up into my chest. When did Jack and Tuna get to be such great mates?

'Oz, I'm up next. Talk to Frog.'

'No, I gotta go. Signal's crock, man!'

Jack started to say something but it was swallowed by static, and then the line went dead. I swore, and for a moment felt like throwing my phone over the wall into the valley. Then I sighed and pushed my earphones back in. I needed some Dead Frank—it was the only thing that would shift the weight pressing on my chest.

Dead Frank's Supersonic Milkfloat were the best band on the planet. They only made two albums before splitting up, but those twenty-five tracks are . . . well . . . beyond words. I just know that whenever I listen to Dead Frank, it makes everything better—even here.

I scrolled through the music on my phone and selected *Spilt Milk*—Dead Frank's seminal debut—and hit *play*. By the time I turned into Scar Hill Lane I was already feeling better. That's the healing power of music, G.

The road up the hillside weaves like coiled spaghetti, which means you end up walking twice as far as you need to. So, when I saw a narrow track branching off and heading straight up the slope, I decided to try it.

After a few minutes the path led into a thick clump of trees. The canopy was so dense, it allowed only splashes of sunlight onto the ground, which is why I didn't see the dog until I was less than ten metres away.

I stopped and tugged my earphones out as the angular head and pointed ears materialized in front of me. It was enormous, G—a beast. I could see muscles flexing underneath the slick black coat, while its eyes held me rooted to the spot. My mouth was suddenly dry and sticky, and the sweat on my back crystallized to a layer of ice.

I took a step backwards and that's when it barked. Though that single word barely does justice to the bloodthirsty eruption of sound that hit me like a shock wave. Teeth flashed as gleaming strings of saliva flicked through the air. I turned, intending to run, but my fear-frozen legs stayed where they were. As I fell, I covered my face with my arms and wondered how much it would hurt when those teeth sank into my flesh.

When nothing happened I looked up and saw that The Beast was no closer than before. It was still barking, jumping up onto its hind legs, then dropping and walking backwards and forwards in tight agitated steps. That's when I noticed the rope attached to its collar, weaving after it in the dirt like a snake.

I sat up and would have laughed, except somebody was already doing it.

The girl looked down at me, still laughing. She was wearing a Crawdale High School uniform, which probably explained why she looked familiar.

'Give you a fright, did he?'

'I tripped . . . ' I said, scrambling to my feet.

'Right.' She nodded and gave one of those smiles people do when they've just seen you make an idiot of yourself. 'It's OK, he won't bite you. Not unless I tell him to, anyhow.' She walked up to The Beast, who rolled over so the girl could scratch its belly.

People say owners resemble their dogs and these two proved it. The girl was tall and broad with long muscular legs, and arms that made mine look thin as string.

'I should get going,' I said, dusting mud from my trousers.

'What you doing here anyhow?' she said. 'You do know you're trespassing?'

'Sorry, I thought it was a short cut,' I said. 'I'm trying to get to Scar Hill Farm.'

'You from that family what just moved in?' She stood up and walked towards me. 'I suppose that makes us neighbours. I'm Isobel Skinner.'

'Oz,' I said. See—friendly, not cocky.

But Isobel wasn't smiling.

That's when I realized where I'd seen her before. Just to be certain, I mentally superimposed a curling moustache and a pair of glasses over Isobel's face, and sure enough there she was—the girl in the picture.

'That would be Oz the artist then,' she said, to make sure we both had a full grasp of the situation.

'Ah . . . yeah . . . um.' I grinned. 'Look, I'm sorry about that. I didn't mean anything . . . personal, you know. It was just a joke, yeah?' My voice trailed off as Isobel said something that sounded like *fun*. I nodded. 'Yeah, that's right. Just a bit of fun.'

She shook her head. 'I said *run*.'

I looked at her.

'Run!' she hissed, walking back towards the dog.

What did she mean, *run*?

Isobel bent down and unclipped the rope from The Beast's collar, and all of a sudden understanding washed over me like a bucket of iced water.

She was holding the dog by its collar with one hand, the rope hanging loose in the other. The Beast, sensing something was about to happen, reared up on its hind legs, dancing from side to side, no longer barking a warning. Now he meant business, the time for talk was over.

Fighting the urge to be sick, cry, or beg for forgiveness—none of which would have helped—I did as Isobel suggested.

And ran.

FOUR

TASTING BURNT RUBBER IN THE AIR

To be honest, G, running's not exactly my thing. Having said that, the motivational effect of forty-two razor-sharp teeth in close proximity to your heels can be quite persuasive.

I could feel The Beast behind me, hear its paws pounding the earth, eating up the space between us. The lane I had so foolishly abandoned earlier lurched into view, but I knew I wouldn't make it. There's only so far that fear and adrenaline can drive an untrained body. Then I saw the trees at the edge of the field—their trunks bent over by the wind. I'd never climbed a tree before, but I reckoned even I should be able to get up one of those. The way I saw it, G—it was my only chance.

I leapt at the nearest one, scrambling and pulling my body up by sheer willpower. I didn't stop climbing until the ground looked a safe distance below. When I finally peered down through the leaves, I expected to see the dog circling the base of the tree, baying and leaping up at me, but there was no sign of it. For a horrible moment I wondered if dogs could climb—but a quick glance around assured me there was nothing hiding in the branches. No dog in the tree. No dog on the ground.

Then I realized.

Isobel had never let go of its collar. She must have been killing herself laughing watching me run. I wondered if she'd seen me climb the tree.

Getting down was probably a good idea, before she or anybody else saw me, but I was wary of going back into the field. Then I spotted the grey stripe of Scar Hill Lane on the other side of the wall below. Some of the branches hung over almost touching it. If I could shuffle along one of those, I should be able to climb out into the lane.

Everything was going fine until the last moment. It must have been my weight, or a freak gust of wind. Whatever the reason—one second I was on the branch, the next I wasn't. It happened so fast I didn't have time to react.

The jagged line of stones on top of the wall broke my fall. I bounced off onto the ground and rolled. For a minute or two I lay on my back in the middle of the road, simply trying to breathe. As the shock wore off, pain stepped in to take its place—hot and sharp. First my knuckles, then my knees. I remembered the phone in my blazer pocket and pulled it out expecting the worst. Thankfully the mobile was unharmed, unlike me and my new school trousers, which had holes in both knees and a tear down one side. Mum was going to kill me.

Then I heard the car.

It took my shaken brain a moment or two to make sense of the sound. A little longer to come to the conclusion that my current position, lying in the middle of the road, probably wasn't the safest place to be.

Needles of pain jabbed at me as I rolled onto my side and tried to get up. I was on one knee when something in the air shifted—a wave of heat—the sour scent of hot metal and oil. A roar filled my ears as the car pounced around the corner and leapt at me, brakes howling, black smoke spitting from its tyres. For a second the driver and I looked at each other, horrified—and then it was gone, passing so close I felt the warmth of its breath on my face. I turned and watched the vehicle swerve out of sight around the bend. I heard a thump, a screech of metal, then everything went quiet—until the delicate sound of fluttering paper broke the silence.

The car had left the road and half embedded itself in the hedge, one back wheel still spinning clear of the tarmac. Its boot had sprung open on impact, spilling postcard sized sheets of paper onto the road, where the wind tossed them skyward into a bizarre paper blizzard.

I hobbled towards the wreckage, tasting burnt rubber in the air, as the driver stumbled out.

'Marcus!'

'Hello, Mum.'

She swerved across the road like the car had done, and dragged me onto the verge.

'Are you all right?' The hand gripping my arm was shaking. 'Are you hurt? Did I hit you?' Mum looked me up and down and gasped, seeing the torn trousers and the blood. 'Oh my God! I did hit you! Where does it hurt?'

'I'm fine. You missed me.'

'You're bleeding,' she said. 'You're probably in shock. We need to call an ambulance. Where's my phone?' Mum fumbled around her skirt for pockets that weren't there.

'Mum! I'm fine. You didn't hit me. I fell out of a tree.'

She stopped searching for her mobile and looked at me. 'What?'

Which is when I realized my mistake.

'What tree? What on earth are you talking about?'

'Um . . . that one!' I pointed.

'What the hell were you doing up a tree?' Mum put a hand to her forehead and closed her eyes, inhaling deeply a couple of times. She does that a lot, usually when she's talking to me or Dad—she says it calms her down, but I'm not sure it works.

'You could have been killed! *I* could have killed you!' Her voice rose to a shriek.

'I got chased by a dog! It was massive!' If I told her about the awful jeopardy I'd been in, maybe she'd go back to being concerned.

'What dog? What are you talking about?'

'This idiot girl set her dog on me!'

'What girl?'

Then again, telling her about Isobel could lead all the way back to the moustache—not a journey I wanted Mum to take.

'I took a short cut and this dog chased me. I had to climb the tree to get away.'

'So where is it now?' Mum peered over the wall into the empty field. 'And what about this girl? You said *an idiot girl set her dog on me*.'

It's scary the way she does that, G. Like she's got some kind of voice recorder inside her head, pre-programmed to remember the stuff you hoped she didn't hear.

'Did I?' I shrugged. 'I thought I saw a girl, but maybe I didn't . . . I don't remember. I think I might be in shock . . . like you said.'

Just then, the wind blew a flurry of paper into us. One of the sheets stuck against my chest. I grabbed it. 'Mum, all your postcards are blowing away.'

She frowned, as though she'd only just noticed the super-sized confetti flapping across the road and over the wall into the field. 'Stay where you are. I'll get them,' she said.

'I can help.'

'No! I don't want you getting run over again.'

'By what? There's no traffic.' We hadn't seen another car since the accident, but Mum insisted I stayed where I was while she collected the spilt postcards.

I sat down on the verge and looked at the piece of paper in my hand. It was a colour photograph of a giant metal wasp. Even though you could see that the insect's abdomen had been constructed from curved strips of painted metal, and the stinger supporting the whole structure was a steel rod, it still made my skin crawl. Flipping the card over, I was confronted by a black and white headshot of my mum looking thoughtful.

Most people's idea of a sculptor is someone who makes bronze statues of dead people for pigeons to sit on, or maybe abstract shapes carved from hunks of stone. Not Mum. She takes old scrap—lawnmowers, garden furniture, bits of engines and cars—and turns them into enormous insects. Which is actually kind of cool—definitely better than the other two options. One of the reasons Mum and Dad bought the old farmhouse was because the two large outbuildings bordering the yard would be perfect for a sculptor's studio. I noticed the address on the postcard read *Scar Hill Studios*—which made it sound a lot more impressive than a pair of leaky old barns.

I was trying to work out where the picture of Mum had been taken, when I heard her cry out. As I looked up, a pile of postcards spilt from her hands and she grabbed her left arm.

'Mum? Are you OK?'

'My arm hurts,' she said, the colour draining from her face as she spoke. 'I must have banged it in the crash. I didn't notice until I tried to use it. But now I can't feel my fingers.'

FIVE

LIKE THE SONG SAYS . . .

The first track on the second album by Dead Frank's Supersonic Milkfloat is called 'Shit Happens'. I thought most people waiting in the Accident and Emergency department of Thackett General Hospital would relate to the sentiment expressed in the lyrics. For a moment I even considered unplugging my headphones and sharing it with them, but decided to send Jack a text instead. He was the one person I knew would truly understand. In fact, I suspected that Jack would find everything that had happened to me that day hilarious.

I'd just clicked *Send* when somebody pulled my earphones out.

'You're supposed to switch your phone *off* in hospitals,' said Meg, dropping into the seat next to me. I should have guessed she would have to get in on the action.

There was nothing like my perfect sister, the superhero—in full Meg-a-Girl mode—to make me look bad. I tell you, G—all she needed was a cape and some lycra.

'What are you doing here?'

Meg ignored me and turned to Dad. 'I left college as soon as I got your text. What's going on? Where's Mum?'

'In with the doctor.'

'Is she all right?'

'They think she might have broken her arm.'

'Broken her arm!' Meg's eyes widened and she looked at me. 'What about you, genius?'

I showed her my collection of dressings and rolled up my ragged trouser leg. 'Five stitches.'

Meg frowned. 'So, remind me. What happened, exactly?'

Of course, we had to go through the whole thing all over again.

'Marcus! Mum could have been killed!' said Meg, when Dad got to the end.

'What about me? *I* could have been killed!'

'Well, if you will go wandering down the middle of the road.'

'I wasn't *wandering* down the middle of the road! I fell out of a tree.'

Meg tucked a strand of hair behind her ear and narrowed her eyes. 'Oh, that's right, I forgot—you were being chased by a dog.'

'Not just a *dog*. This thing was like the Hound of the Baskervilles!'

'Really? What was it? A poodle? A Scottie? Or a really big chihuahua?' She snorted. 'So why did it chase you, Marcus? What did *you* do?'

'Me?'

Meg raised an eyebrow.

'How should I know? Maybe it didn't like the look of me. Maybe it was hungry. I didn't stick around to find out.'

'If there's a dangerous dog on the loose we ought to report it,' Dad said, and alarms went off in my head.

I had to make the whole thing sound like a stupid accident. 'I took a short cut and got lost. I was probably trespassing or something. Look—I know it was my fault—and I'm sorry.'

'You don't say!' said Meg.

'Anyway, none of this would have happened if we'd stayed in Hardacre,' I said. 'I mean, there must be less trees per square metre in a town, so statistically the chances of falling out of one are greatly reduced. It's simple maths.'

Dad sighed and shook his head. 'What I don't understand, is why things like this always happen to you, Oz. It's like the milkfloat all over again.'

I couldn't help smiling at the memory. It had been Jack's idea. We were only planning to take some pictures—recreate the Dead Frank's cover for *Spilt Milk*. I just jumped in the driver's seat so Jack could take my photo. I didn't mean to set the thing going, but like the song says—sometimes *shit happens*.

When Mum came out with her arm in a sling, the first thing she asked was if I was OK.

'I'm fine. Just five stitches in my knee. What about your arm?'

She shrugged. 'It'll mend. At least you're still here.' I heard her voice catch as she put her good arm around my bruised shoulders and squeezed so hard it took an effort not to cry out. 'Stupid boy!' She sniffed. 'I keep seeing you there in the middle of the road and I just know I'm going to hit you.'

'But you didn't,' said Dad. 'Come on. Let's go home.'

There are only three seats in the front of Dad's van, so I was in the back. It's dark and noisy with all the lengths of pipe and tools rattling about, but I like it. I climbed into the bath that will be in our house once Dad gets around to swapping it for the stained and cracked one we have currently. For the time being, it made a more comfortable seat than the floor. I lay back and closed my eyes as every bump in the road mapped a different bruise on my body. I could hear my family talking in the cab, but I wasn't really listening until Mum said:

'I was on my way back from a meeting with Geraint at the Sculpture Park. He offered me a show.'

'That's fantastic,' said Dad.

'Yes, it would have been quite an opportunity. Of course I'll have to cancel now.'

'Why? When is it?'

'December. But I need at least three new pieces for the main hall. I was going to have to work flat out as it was to get everything ready in time. There's no way I'll be able to do it with only one good arm.'

'Can't he put the date back a few months?'

'No. I only got the slot because the original artist pulled out and I said I could be ready at short notice.' She sighed. 'Why else do you think they asked? I wouldn't get a sniff at a place like that normally.'

'Oh, Mum, I'm so sorry,' said Meg.

'What about if I helped?' Dad said. 'At least it's your left arm. You can still do all the clever stuff. I don't mind being your studio slave!' He laughed.

'You're busy enough as it is,' said Mum. 'No. It would have been nice, but it doesn't matter. The important thing is that my boy's still in one piece.'

Meg turned round and looked at me over the back of the seat. I didn't need to be able to see her face to read her expression.

Shit happens, I told myself. But why does it always have to happen to me?

SIX

OMG

I felt like I'd spent the night in a washing machine on spin cycle—or maybe recently fallen out of a tree. My stitches were tight and itchy, and it was hard to tell where one ache finished and the next began. The doctor at the hospital had said I should take a day off school to rest and give the wound a chance to heal. I meant to stay in bed, sleep through to the afternoon, but the gnawing in my knee woke me up at some ridiculously early hour.

'The birdman lives,' said Dad, as I flopped down next to Meg on the sofa in the kitchen. 'How you feeling, matey?'

'Everything hurts,' I said. 'I've got pains in places I didn't know I had places.'

'Want some tea?' Dad believed tea could cure all ailments.

I shook my head. 'Where's Mum?'

'In bed,' said Dad. 'I rang the college and told them she wouldn't be in today.'

'Will she lose her job?'

'Shouldn't think so. She'll still be able to impart knowledge with only one good arm!'

Meg swore and slammed down her phone. 'Why is there never a reception in this bloody place! It keeps dropping out!'

'That'll be the hills, love,' said Dad. 'Not a lot we can do about that.'

'Except live somewhere else.' She stood up. 'I'm going for a bath, though I don't suppose there'll be any hot water.'

Dad raised his eyebrows. 'Think I might make myself scarce. If there's no hot water, it'll be my fault.' He reached into the baggy side pocket of his shorts and pulled out a vast bunch of keys. 'I'd better go and see if I can extract your mum's car from that hedge before someone tows it away. Try not to kill yourself while I'm gone, eh, mate.'

Try not to kill yourself. That was the plan.

With Mum in bed and Meg in the bath, I decided to take the opportunity for a few rounds of *SlamShowdown*.

I was fighting a skinny girl called *Raven Rock*, whose special move was using her ponytail as a whip. It had a stone at the end which could do some damage if you didn't get out of the way—but seriously, all you had to do was duck, then attack while the ponytail was on the backward arc of its rotation. Easy.

I was well on the way to a new high score when the sofa vibrated beneath me, followed by a muffled *ding*.

I can't have taken my eyes off the screen for more than a second before I heard the groan of the electronic crowd. When I looked back, the game version of me was lying on the ground, while the letters KO revolved in the air and *Raven Rock* did a stupid victory dance over my battered body.

I threw down the controller in disgust and snatched up the vibrating cushion that had distracted me. Meg's mobile was underneath, the display flashing to signal a new message had arrived. So much for no reception.

'She's not here,' I told the phone. 'Gone to spread her joy elsewhere.'

I turned my attention back to the game, but when the mobile went off for the third time I gave up. I decided to see who was responsible for ruining my score and thought it might be a laugh to text back pretending to be Meg. Getting into my sister's phone wasn't a problem, I'd worked out her password ages ago.

The unread messages were all from Meg's best friend, Chloe. Big surprise.

Some time during Year Eleven, Chloe had taken Meg on a demonstration march in London. Before she went, I think my sister would have struggled to name the Prime Minister. A week later, she was ranting at the TV news and lecturing Mum about the coffee she drinks. For a few months none of us could buy, wear, drink, or eat anything without Meg telling us we were personally responsible for poverty, deforestation, or exploitation of slaves.

Some of the time she actually talked some sense, and between you and me, G, I even stopped buying certain brands—but I wasn't going to tell Meg that. It was too easy to wind her up. I started making jokes about her being some kind of eco superhero, which was how Meg-a-Girl was born. Then one day, she suddenly stopped taking the bait. Every time I said anything, she'd just sniff and accuse me of male oppression, or infringement of her human rights, which took all the fun out of it, to be honest.

I selected the first message in the list so I could send a reply.

OMG

R u sure?

I rolled my eyes. Meg and Chloe existed in a state of perpetual crisis. I wondered what this latest one was.

I opened the next message in the list.

Does K know?

I wondered who K was. All Meg's friends used stupid abbreviations of their names—K was probably Keira, or Kirsty or . . . Kermit the Frog, for all I knew.

Wot u going 2 do? Here 4 u hon xx

That one made me laugh out loud. I scrolled down the conversation history to find out quite how pathetic my sister was being this time.

Meg: My life is over. (See what I mean?)

Chloe: Oh, honey! wots wrng?

M: Everything

C: Moving away? Yeh. Sucks. Miss u alreddy

M: And the rest.

C: ?

M: Don't tell anyone

C: ???!

M: Promise?

C: I promise. What is it?

M: I'm pregnant.

C: OMG. R u sure? (Which is where I came in.)

I stared at the screen not quite believing what I saw. Then I read it again, just to be sure. Just in case there was any other way of reading this. There wasn't.

Meg was pregnant.

My seventeen-year-old big sister was going to have a baby.

OMG and then some!

I jumped when the phone vibrated in my hand as a further message arrived. It was Chloe again.

Megan? R U there?

My finger hovered over the *reply* option, but suddenly I couldn't think of anything to say. And then I sensed that I was no longer alone in the room.

SEVEN

EATING CUSHION

I'd been caught. In the face of such indisputable evidence, G, there was only one option—

I turned and held out the mobile. 'I found your phone,' I said—my widest, innocent-little-brother smile fixed on my face.

'Thanks, mate!' said Dad. 'But that's not mine.'

'Sorry! I thought you were Meg.'

Dad grunted. 'She wouldn't thank you for that.' He walked over to the sink and washed his hands, talking to me over his shoulder. 'You'll be pleased to know your mother's car doesn't look too bad. The damage is mainly cosmetic. Should be back on the road in a couple of weeks.'

I nodded as a fresh bucket-load of guilt emptied over me. 'I'll pay . . . you know . . . for the parts.'

'Oh, I'm sure you'll end up paying for it, mate!' Dad laughed, drying his hands as he walked towards me. 'You haven't seen my bog book have you?'

'Your what?'

'That catalogue with all the bathroom stuff in it. I need to order the new throne.'

I shook my head.

'I'm sure I filed it round here somewhere.' Dad poked through a pile of papers balanced on top of the fridge.

While his back was turned, I took the opportunity to reset Chloe's texts as *unopened* and put Meg's phone back under the cushion. She'd never know.

But I would.

I couldn't stop thinking about it. My self-righteous, do-gooding, superhero sister had got herself knocked-up! In one simple act, Meg had managed to eclipse anything bad I could ever do. Even breaking Mum's arm would seem like nothing compared to this.

My brain was still attempting to process the information when Meg walked into the kitchen. She was wearing her dressing gown and a pair of white Dr Marten boots—nobody ever went barefoot in the house. Dad had thought the old carpets might be responsible for the open grave smell that haunted the place, so he ripped them out. Unfortunately it hadn't solved the problem and now, as well as the worms that wriggled up between the stone flags in the hallway and the kitchen, the exposed ancient floorboards upstairs were a minefield of jagged splinters, rusty nails, and hundred-year-old grit.

'This just came out of the tap,' said Meg, handing something to Dad and folding her arms.

'Looks like a frog's leg,' he said. 'Wonder where the rest of him went?'

'Surely the question is, why are amphibian body parts coming out of our taps?'

'All part of the charm of living in the country, my Angel Delight!'

'Tell me we're going to have a new bathroom soon!' said Meg, sounding almost tearful.

'I'm working on that very thing,' Dad said. 'Only I seem to have mislaid my plumbing catalogue.'

Meg crouched down and picked something off the floor. 'This one?'

'Of course!' Dad clapped the flat of his hand to his forehead. 'Floor for plumbing. Fridge for electrics. Can't even remember my own filing system!' He grinned. 'Right! I'm off. Gotta see a man about a bog!'

He was still chuckling as he closed the back door, leaving me alone in the kitchen with Meg.

'What are you staring at?' she said, before I realized I was.

'Just wondering which evil corporation you were going to bring down today. By the way, have you thought any more about that cape?'

Meg rolled her eyes and reached into the cupboard for a bowl.

The truth was, G—I couldn't drag my eyes away from her. I thought I'd be able to tell—that she would look different somehow. But she didn't.

Maybe she wasn't pregnant? Perhaps I'd come in at the end of a conversation and misunderstood. It wasn't like I could just ask her. At least, not in so many words . . .

I reached under the cushion and held up her phone. 'You left this,' I said. 'It keeps going off. I got my ass kicked by *Raven Rock* because of it!'

Meg snorted. 'Meanwhile back in the real world,' she said, taking it from me, her fingers already racing across the keys. Then her head snapped around. 'Did you touch this?'

'Of course I touched it. I just gave it to you.'

'Did you read it?'

'Read it?' If in doubt always answer a question with a question, G. It buys you time. 'Why would I be interested in anything you and your mates are talking about?'

She knew I was lying, because I've been lying to Meg my whole life and she always knows. She glanced at the screen in her hand, then back at me, and I saw something in her eyes. Doubt? Fear? Anger?

I wasn't going to say anything, but I just couldn't help myself. 'So . . . I suppose congratulations are in order.'

Meg frowned.

'I mean, I thought I couldn't be beaten, but I've got to hand it to you, sis. You've really raised the bar on this one.' I was looking for a sign—a reaction—something that would prove my suspicions were correct.

Finding myself pinned to the sofa with Meg kneeling on my chest probably counts.

'Shut up!' she said, jamming a cushion over my face. 'You don't know what you're talking about!'

I tried to reply, but it's hard to talk when you're being force fed soft furnishings. I twisted my head to one side. 'I saw the text! You're pregnant!'

Meg glanced towards the doorway, then lowered her mouth and hissed into my ear. 'You made a mistake.' Her breath was hot against my face. 'Understand?'

I got the impression that my sister wasn't in the mood to talk about her news just yet. Her knees were digging into my bruised ribs and it was getting hard to breathe. There are occasions, G, when a tactical retreat is the wisest option. So I nodded—and after a few seconds Meg released her grip. I sat up coughing and spitting, picking bits of fluff from my tongue and trying not to think about how many people had sat and farted on that cushion.

Meg had just climbed off me when the back door opened and Dad burst in. 'Always helps to take some money when you go shopping,' he said, grabbing his wallet from the fruit bowl. He shook his head, waved and walked back outside. When I turned round, Meg had gone.

EIGHT

'LIKE POKING A WASPS' NEST WITH A STICK'

My sister's recent revelation was momentarily pushed to one side by the harsh reality of a return to Crawdale High. Despite the fact that my knee ached as though there was a hungry rat gnawing on it, my caring parents insisted on thrusting me into my scuffed and blood-stained blazer, and sending me back to school.

I knew something was going on the moment I saw the crowd gathered in the corridor. It parted to let me through, so I could benefit from the full impact of the enormous pair of yellow Y-fronts taped to the front of my locker. Everyone's eyes were fixed on me, waiting to see how I would react.

'There you go, Kecks,' said Gareth. 'Proper bloke's undercracker that. None of your lacy southern nonsense!'

'Thanks.' I tried to sound bored, as though finding giant, custard-coloured undies stuck to my locker was an everyday experience. 'Are you sure *you* don't need them any more though?' I was fairly sure Gareth was responsible, but I also suspected that any attempts at retribution on my part would end badly—with me being forced to eat the pants or wear them as a hat.

I stepped forward and peeled the underwear off my locker, trying to touch as little of the fabric as possible, then threw them inside and slammed the door. When I turned round Isobel Skinner was smirking at me from the far end of the corridor.

In that instant, all the frustration and humiliation boiling inside me focused itself on her. I found myself walking towards her, even though I had no idea what I was going to do, or say, when I got there. I was so blind with rage, that I didn't see the person crouching by one of the floor-level lockers, until I tripped over him.

'Sorry!' The kid looked up and I saw it was Ryan.

I scowled. 'What are you *doing* down there?'

'It's my locker!'

'Oh . . . right. Yeah.' I glanced back down the corridor, but Isobel Skinner had gone. I swore.

'What's wrong?' Ryan closed his locker and stood up.

'Nothing . . . I just wanted to have a word with Isobel Skinner.'

His eyes widened. 'Psycho Skinner! What d'you want *her* for?'

'I wanted to thank her for these.' I rolled up my trouser leg and showed him my stitches.

Ryan winced. 'She did that?'

'Well, sort of . . . it was her fault anyway.'

'Is that why you weren't at school yesterday?'

I nodded, then found myself telling him everything that had happened—the whole dog, tree, car fiasco. I think I just needed to tell someone the truth. The strange thing was, Ryan appeared to believe me. In fact, he didn't seem at all surprised.

'There's a reason we call her *Psycho*,' he said. 'I tried to warn you—when you drew that moustache.'

I shrugged. 'It was just a moustache and some glasses!'

'Yeah, on *Psycho Skinner's face*!'

'So?'

Ryan shook his head. 'Drawing that moustache on Psycho's picture . . . ' he frowned, 'it was like poking a wasps' nest with a stick. No—poking a wasps' nest with a stick while covered in strawberry jam.' He looked at me, huge eyes peering through the twists of hair. 'You want to be careful,' he said. 'Everyone round here knows the Skinners are nutters. You don't want to get on the wrong side of them.'

'What are they, like the local sheep rustling mafia or something?' I laughed.

'Pretty much,' said Ryan, his face completely serious. 'I don't know about the sheep part, but if there's something dodgy going on round here, there's usually a Skinner involved.'

'Right.'

'You know she does tae-kwon-do,' he said, as we headed for registration.

'Who?'

'Psycho. She's a black belt. County Champion. At least she was until she got banned for being too violent!' Ryan's eyebrows were going crazy. 'She beat the crap out of some bloke—broke his jaw. They reckon he said something to her, but she smashed him up so bad, it was ages before he could tell anybody.' He glanced around before continuing in a hushed voice. 'And get this! Now she has to go and see a psychiatrist once a week to deal with her—*anger management issues*!' His fingers made a set of inverted commas in the air.

I remembered the look in Isobel's eyes when she told me to run. I mean, who except a complete nutter would threaten someone with a dog?

'I heard she's on pills,' said Ryan, 'you know, to keep it under control. She's like the Incredible Hulk—perfectly normal until she gets angry, and then—' He mimed an explosion with his hands and when he spoke again his voice was deeper, eyes wild. 'Don't make me angry. You wouldn't like me when I'm angry.'

I stared at him.

'The Incredible Hulk?' he said. 'You know—big green bloke—always bursting out of his clothes.'

'Yeah, I know who the Hulk is.' So Ryan was one of those nerdy comic kids. I should have guessed.

'Good, because it's important you know what you're dealing with,' said Ryan. He grinned and put a hand on my shoulder. 'But don't worry, I've got your back.'

'O . . . K . . . um . . . thanks,' I said.

I bet he did Yoda impressions too.

I took Ryan's promise to *watch my back* as just another movie quote he liked the sound of. But when he kept appearing—in the corridor between lessons and in the queue for the canteen—I realized he was serious. I tried ignoring him but it didn't seem to make any difference.

Don't get me wrong, G—Ryan was OK, I just didn't want him as my new best friend. He was like a walking radio, pouring out a constant stream of random lines from films and facts about comic characters I'd never heard of. After my Pete Taylor incident, I had a lot of ground to make up. I was never going to shake the *Kecks* tag if I became part of some tragic double-act with Ryan.

When I saw him waiting to catch the bus home, I kept out of sight until he got on—then sat at the front, next to some old woman.

As we drove into the hills it started raining. The valley disappeared from view. All I could see was the road and the craggy stone walls smothered in mist. I watched the huge wipers at the front of the bus sloshing back and forth across the screen. Every so often they synced with the music in my ears, and for a few bars kept time with Dead Frank. It wasn't long before the hypnotic effect of watching them and the motion of the bus was making my eyelids droop.

When the old woman I was sitting next to poked me in the ribs, I opened my eyes and realized my head was on her shoulder. I sat up blushing and pulled my earphones out.

'We've got to get off!' she said.

'Where are we? Have I missed Slowleigh?' I remembered to pronounce it *Slowel*.

The woman frowned. 'No. Bus is jiggered.'

'What?'

'Broke down.' She shook her head. 'You'll have to wait for next one.'

We had stopped in a village. There was a pub and some houses, even a pavement of sorts, but no shelter. The rain cut horizontal lines through the grey landscape, while the wind whipped and tugged at my clothes.

'When's the next bus?' I asked.

'Won't be another one to Slowleigh while an hour, love!' said the woman, fighting her way into a long plastic mac.

'An hour!'

She shrugged. 'You could walk it quicker.'

Walk it! She must be mad. My knee throbbed like an angry pit-bull and my trousers were soaked already. I found my mobile and dialled Dad, but it was Meg who answered.

'Where's Dad?'

'Hello, Oz, how are you?'

'Yeah, yeah, hello—where's Dad?'

'Gone out.'

'Gone out! Where?'

'He's doing some plumbing for that builder in Thackett, I think.'

I swore. 'The bus broke down! There's not another one for an hour. And it's raining.'

Meg laughed. I probably would have done the same in her position, but at that moment I wasn't in the mood to see the funny side. Which is why I said:

'So anyway, Meg—how's the baby today?'

I wasn't surprised when she swore at me and slammed the phone down. Of course when I called back, she didn't pick up.

I had no choice but to wait for the replacement horse and cart to turn up—if I didn't drown first.

I was about to put my earphones back in when someone tapped me on the shoulder. It took a moment to recognize the face grinning inside the fur-trimmed hood.

'I thought it was you!' said Ryan. 'You can wait at mine if you like.'

'What?'

'I only live over there.' He pointed towards a row of narrow grey houses on the opposite side of the road. 'You'll be able to see the bus coming from my window.'

NINE

KIND OF IMPRESSIVE

Ryan opened the front door and shouted into the house. 'Grandad! I've brought a friend home!' I winced, then reminded myself that it had to be better than waiting an hour in the rain.

I heard the sound of a television being turned off, and then a figure appeared at the end of the hallway. He had the same pointed features and blue eyes as Ryan, but was completely bald. What his head lacked, his chin made up for in abundance. A thick silver beard flowed from his face, ending in a point midway down his stomach. I noticed he was wearing a black *Lord of the Rings* T-shirt, with a picture of Gandalf the wizard partially obscured by the blanket of whiskers.

'Ah!' he said—and then a stream of words of which *Ryan* was the only one I understood. I sensed he was waiting for an answer.

'I'm Oz,' I said, thinking it would be a safe option.

Unfortunately, it only encouraged the old man to further conversation. More words I couldn't make out, then a chuckle, at which point he looked down and tapped his chest.

Ryan shook his head. 'No, his name's Osbourne, Grandad—but people call him Oz.' He turned to me. 'He thought you were named after the wizard—you know, the Wizard of Oz.'

Ryan's grandad nodded and pointed to his T-shirt.

'Right,' I said, thinking *he* looked more like a wizard than I did.

I followed them into a narrow room overlooking the street. A huge flat-screen TV stood at one end, with two worn leather armchairs angled to face it. An entire wall was taken up with shelves crammed full of DVDs. It conjured a vision of Ryan and his grandad sitting in the chairs watching movies together every evening. Which would explain a lot.

'I see you like your films then,' I said.

Ryan shrugged. 'It's just *A to L* in here, the rest are upstairs with the *Sci-Fi*, *World Cinema* and *TV Series*. If you want to borrow anything, just ask.'

OK—so Ryan lived in Blockbuster with Grandalf the Wizard. So far, so weird.

But however strange it was downstairs, G, I still wasn't prepared for the sight that greeted me when Ryan opened his bedroom door.

I think I swore. I'm pretty sure I made some kind of sound, because Ryan looked at me really quickly and then blushed redder than a traffic light.

It was kind of impressive . . . but for all the wrong reasons. Every available space on the walls and ceiling was covered in pictures: film posters, comic books, superheroes, hobbits and goblins, scantily-clad women with big swords, bearded men toting shiny guns. There were drawings too, diagrams of futuristic weapons and spacecraft; strange hybrid faces; costumes and armour. I didn't even notice the display case at first, even though it must have contained over a hundred hand-painted plastic figures.

'Wow!' I couldn't think what else to say.

A pinboard above Ryan's bed had pictures of people in fancy dress stuck to it. I guessed they were supposed to be characters from a film—*Lord of the Rings* probably. There was someone dressed as a goblin—posing in a wood with an axe in one hand and a bottle of beer in the other. Another showed some bloke with a bow and arrow kneeling in front of a woman wearing a long white dress with enormous sleeves. The fact you could see her Nike trainers poking out underneath kind of spoilt the effect. I spotted Ryan's grandad, looking scarily like the real Gandalf, and then . . .

'Is that you?' I peered more closely at the photograph of the boy sitting under a tree holding a sword. He was wearing a hooded cloak and shorts and . . . 'What's that on your feet?'

'Hobbit socks,' mumbled Ryan. 'I . . . made them myself.'

I wasn't quite sure what to do with my face.

'Want some music on?' he said quickly, crouching down next to an old-fashioned stereo system and a stack of LPs.

I dragged my eyes away from the photo. 'Is that vinyl?'

Ryan nodded. 'Most of these were my mum's. I bought the rest from charity shops and that. Do you like the Beatles? I've got lots of Beatles.' He raised the lid on the ancient turntable and lifted the arm onto the disc of black plastic. There was a pop, a hiss and crackle, then a warped voice counting, before music burst from the speakers.

'*Revolver*,' said Ryan, chewing his lip. 'It's the best one I think. That or *Rubber Soul*.'

I frowned. 'I'm not much into the Beatles. I think my dad likes them.'

'Right.' Ryan nodded. He picked up the record sleeve and stared at it for ages, as if he was looking for something hidden in the picture.

I thumbed through the stack of CDs next to the stereo, but they weren't much better. Mostly *Now* compilations and a few of those really obvious chart albums you can buy in supermarkets for a fiver. It was kind of depressing.

I sat back on my heels. 'You heard any Dead Frank's Supersonic Milkfloat?'

Ryan frowned and shook his head.

'Cigarette UFO?'

'Nope.'

'Prayer for Halo? Surely, you've heard "Love me like you kill me!"'

'Don't think so. What's it go like?'

'Seriously? Where have you been, man?' I sighed and pulled out my phone. 'Here—listen to this.' I passed him my earphones and selected the opening track from *Spilt Milk*.

Ryan stroked his chin as he listened, his face serious behind the curtain of hair. When the song finished, he handed back the mobile. 'What did you say they were called again?'

'Dead Frank's Supersonic Milkfloat. Amazing, yeah?'

Ryan shrugged. 'Different.' He reached over and turned the volume back up on the Beatles. 'Do you want something to eat?'

How could he dismiss Dead Frank after one track? Especially in favour of the Beatles! And what did he mean—*different*? This bedroom—now *that* was different!

Ryan went downstairs and I wondered if there was time to call Jack. I had to tell him about this place! Only I doubted he'd believe me unless he saw it for himself. Then I remembered what I was holding.

I took a dozen shots of Ryan's room with my phone: the pinboard above the bed; the antique vinyl turntable with the Beatles record sleeve on top; the display case of figures; then a few close-ups of Ryan dressed as a hobbit with his little sword and hairy-feet socks. Jack was going to choke when he saw these—talk about *different*!

When Ryan came back into the room carrying two cans of Coke and a plate of biscuits, I was innocently flicking through his records.

TEN

FOAM SHRIMP ALIEN

By the time I limped up the track to the farm, even Dead Frank was struggling to distract me from the siren of pain blaring in my knee. It was dark. The only light came from the windows of Mum's studio, spilling stripes of yellow across the wet cobbles. As I reached the gate something large stepped from the shadows, bringing me to an abrupt halt. I stared—hand on the latch—while my brain fumbled for a reason to explain why Psycho Skinner's dog was standing in our yard.

'You're late!' I looked up and saw Mum strolling towards me. 'Don't mind Lucky,' she said. 'He won't hurt you. Will you, beautiful?' The Beast wagged its tail as she scratched behind its ears, but didn't take its eyes off me. I could tell what it was thinking: *You and me. We got unfinished business, boy!*

I was about to tell Mum that this was the phantom hound that had caused the accident, when Psycho Skinner herself appeared in the studio doorway. She was clutching the carcass of an old lawnmower.

'Where d'you want this, Mrs Osbourne?' she said, then noticed me and her face changed.

'Oh . . . stick it on the dismantle pile . . . and call me Dawn. Mrs Osbourne sounds so old!' Mum laughed.

'What's *she* doing here?' I hissed, keeping the gate between me and The Beast.

'Isobel? She lives next door.'

'So why is she here and not next door, then? Did she get lost on her way home?'

Mum frowned. 'She was taking Lucky for a walk and saw me struggling to move some things. She offered to help.'

Why would Psycho Skinner offer to help anyone—especially my mum?

'She's been brilliant,' said Mum, crouching down to give The Beast another scratch. 'I wanted to sort through some of my old work, to see if there was anything I could use for the exhibition. Your dad was going to help, but he's been busy on that job in Thackett. I tried to do it on my own, but I wasn't getting on too well until Isobel showed up.'

Something metallic clanged in the barn, followed by the sound of a heavy object being dragged across the floor. What was Psycho doing in there? I wondered if I should warn Mum that she had a certified lunatic loose in her studio. Then again, my information on the Skinners had come from Ryan, whose grip on reality seemed slippery at best. Perhaps Isobel *had* simply stopped to help. Plus . . . I really didn't want to make her angry.

I was in my room in the attic when the power went off. I felt my way down the steps and found Meg on the landing.

'What's going on?'

'Slight technical hitch! No need to be alarmed.' Dad's voice floated up the stairs. 'Normal service will be resumed as soon as possible,' he said, appearing from the gloom and handing me a torch. 'Until then you might need this.'

'This place is a joke,' muttered Meg, walking back into her bedroom.

I followed and sat down on the end of the bed.

'Don't sit, you're not staying.'

I ignored her and shone the torch around the room. I was impressed. We'd been in the house for less than a month and already Meg's room had achieved the kind of lived-in squalor it usually took years to perfect. It looked as though her wardrobe had exploded, spreading clothes like shrapnel onto every available surface. 'I like what you've done with the place,' I said.

Meg stood in front of me, hands on hips. 'Was there something you wanted, Oz?'

'No. Just hanging with my big sis.' I grinned up at her. 'So, what do you think of it so far?' I expected Meg to tell me to leave, but after a moment she sighed and climbed into bed.

'College is a joke,' she said. 'The tutors don't know what they're doing and my Sociology syllabus is completely different to the one I started at school—so I'm miles behind.' She folded her arms. 'The extra-curricular options are non-existent. I enquired about a student newspaper and they looked at me like I'd asked to start an arsonists' club! Whenever I speak to anyone it's like we're talking completely different languages.'

'I get that!' I said. 'Today right, this kid was trying to tell me something and I didn't have a clue what he was saying. So I was like, yeah—great! Turned out his dog had got run over this morning!'

Meg laughed, then covered her mouth with a hand. 'Sorry, that's not funny.'

'He didn't think so either.' I leant back on the bed and something sharp poked into my elbow. When I picked up the object, I saw it was a book.

'Hey! Give me that!' Meg made a lunge for it, but I jumped off the bed out of reach.

'Don't snatch! What is it anyway?' I moved the torch to illuminate the cover. '*Baby's Journey*,' I read. '*A day-to-day guide to your pregnancy*.' I stopped and swung the light towards my sister. 'So . . . about that text. The one where you told Chloe you were pregnant.'

Meg shielded her eyes from the light.

I shone the torch back to the book. 'I may not be Sherlock Holmes, but I'd say this was fairly strong evidence. Unless you're just really interested in babies all of a sudden.'

My sister didn't answer. Just sat and picked at the edge of her duvet.

'Look, I won't tell anyone, but seriously, Meg—a baby!'

'I know! You think that hasn't crossed my mind? Jesus! I've hardly slept since I found out.'

'So what are you going to do?'

'I don't know!'

'Have you told Mum and Dad?'

She snorted. 'What do *you* think? I'm still breathing aren't I?'

'You're going to have to tell them eventually though. I mean, don't you think they'll notice a baby around the place?'

'Oz! I know!'

I sat down again and opened the book. 'What is all this stuff?' There was a drawing in the corner of each page—like a flick book. The first one showed a pink blob with crinkly edges—like those foam shrimp sweets you can get. A few pictures further on, the thing began to morph into an alien with a bulbous head and big black eyes.

'So, is that . . . what you've got in there?' I shone the torch onto her belly.

'I suppose.'

I found myself staring at her again, trying to imagine the Foam Shrimp Alien growing inside, but I couldn't. She just looked like my sister—the same as always.

'What's it feel like?'

'I don't know. It doesn't feel like anything.'

I turned a couple more pages until I reached one entitled *Birth: The day you have been waiting for.* There were lots of photos of pregnant women pulling faces and blokes looking scared. The next page showed a series of new-born babies—the funny thing was, they looked like aliens again, all wrinkly and covered in slime.

I laughed. 'That one looks like Gonzo from *The Muppets*!' I pointed to a particularly ugly blue baby with bulging eyes. 'Imagine if yours came out looking like that!'

Meg snatched the book and snapped it shut. 'Time's up, Oz! Get lost!'

'Hang on a minute!' Something had just occurred to me. I don't know why I hadn't thought of it before. But that page of scared looking dads had reminded me of something Chloe had written in her text. *Does K know?*

K was Kris! Kris-with-a-K! He'd been Meg's boyfriend for about six months before we left Hardacre, but the few times she'd brought him home I'd been at Jack's, so we never met. Which might explain why I'd forgotten he existed.

'So what did Kris say when you told him?'

I felt Meg tense and then she shrugged. 'Nothing.'

'*Nothing*? He must have said something . . . unless he fainted! Is that what happened?'

'No, Oz, he didn't faint.'

'So what happened when you told him?'

Meg gnawed on her thumbnail but didn't answer.

'You did tell him?'

She looked at me.

'You mean he doesn't know?'

Meg shook her head.

I swore, then started laughing.

'It's not funny, Oz!'

'I know. I'm sorry. It's just . . . seriously, Meg! Why didn't you tell him?'

'Because we broke up! Idiot!'

I remembered that I actually knew this. Meg's break-up had featured heavily in the weeks prior to our departure. 'So you split up and *then* found out you were pregnant.'

'Well done, Sherlock!' Meg gave a sarcastic round of applause.

'And now you're pregnant with your ex-boyfriend's baby.'

She nodded. 'You're on fire tonight, little brother.'

'Man! That is seriously messed up!'

Meg didn't answer. When I looked across, I saw the gleam of tears in her eyes, and had the feeling that show and tell was over for the night.

ELEVEN

SERIOUSLY SCARY

The next morning Ryan got on the bus and handed me a pair of DVDs. 'You should watch these,' he said, 'so you know what you're dealing with.'

'*The Godfather*?'

'It's a classic,' said Ryan. 'Probably the best gangster film ever made.' He pointed to the second case. 'And that's a British version—sort of.' The film was called *Lock, Stock and Two Smoking Barrels*. 'It's set down in London where you're from. Dead funny.'

'Um . . . thanks.' I didn't know what else to say and wondered if I should mention the fact that Psycho Skinner had been at my house the previous evening.

It was even harder not to tell Ryan about Meg. The knowledge had been bouncing around in my head for days now. I'd already sent Jack a text, but he'd been more interested in giving me the lowdown on some hilarious incident involving Frog, Tuna, and Libby Marshall's pencil case. His last text had ended with the immortal words—*You should have been there, man*.

That night, I watched *The Godfather* on my laptop in bed. To be honest it was a bit boring, especially at the start, but I stuck with it. There had to be a reason everyone thought it was *a classic*. It's about this gangster boss called Don Corleone. His family are at war with a load of other mafia families. Basically they spend the whole film talking and trying to kill each other. One bloke wakes up to find a horse's head in bed with him, which was kind of gruesome.

It took me ages to get to sleep afterwards and then I dreamt that Psycho Skinner came into my room riding a horse without a head. I spent the rest of the night with the light on.

Halfway through dinner on Saturday night Mum's mobile went off. When she came back to the table five minutes later, she was smiling.

'Good news?' said Dad.

'That was Jane from the White Gallery. She's agreed to lend me the six pieces from their collection for the exhibition.'

'Fantastic!'

'I found a few old ones in the barn too,' said Mum, picking up her fork. 'With Isobel's help I'll be able to make the mantis, plus modify some of the older sculptures. If all goes to plan I should be ready in time, even with this.' She raised her cast and grinned.

'Now *that* deserves a celebratory pudding!' said Dad. 'Go and grab that box of Cornettos out of the freezer, Oz!'

I didn't move. My mind was fixed on something Mum had said.

'What do you mean? *With Isobel's help*.'

'Didn't I tell you? She's going to come and work with me. Be my extra arm!'

'Work with you?'

'That's right. I'm going to pay her to be my assistant. Not that she asked for money, but it wouldn't feel right otherwise.' Mum smiled. 'She was so helpful the other day and seemed genuinely interested in what I was doing. When I mentioned the idea of a more permanent arrangement, she jumped at the chance. To be honest I think she enjoys the time away from the house. From what I can gather things have been quite tough at home since her mum left.'

'Isobel Skinner?'

'Yes, Marcus! Isobel Skinner.' She frowned. 'What's wrong with you?'

What was wrong with me? For a start I couldn't believe Psycho had the nerve to take money off Mum for helping, when there wouldn't be any need if she hadn't threatened me with The Beast. But what really made me mad was the fact I couldn't say anything. The moment I told Mum about Psycho's involvement in the accident, she'd find out about the moustache and I'd get into even more trouble.

I was so frustrated by what I couldn't say, that I blurted out: 'You know the Skinners are like the local mafia round here—like that family in *The Godfather*.' Yeah, I know, it sounded stupid to me too. But if I'm honest, G, watching that film had got me spooked. I mean, what if Ryan *was* telling the truth?

Dad laughed, then stopped abruptly. 'Hang on, when did *you* see *The Godfather*?'

'The point is,' I said, avoiding the question. 'They're like seriously scary.' I relayed what Ryan had told me about the Skinner family, finishing off with, 'Isobel has to take pills to stop her from going crazy. Mum's lucky she didn't beat her to death with one of her own sculptures.'

Mum looked annoyed. 'Don't be so ridiculous, Marcus! I'm disappointed. I'd have thought you'd know better than to listen to schoolyard gossip. I hope you haven't been repeating this to anyone. The Skinners are our neighbours.'

'How do you know it's not true?'

'I know Isobel and I trust my own instincts—especially over malicious rumours.'

For some reason Dad seemed to find the whole thing hilarious. 'I take it you haven't heard your sister's news then!'

I looked across the table at Meg. *She'd told them?*

My sister shook her head, her eyes flashing a warning. 'No, I haven't told Oz about my job yet.'

'Job?'

'Meg's going to be working at the pub in the village,' said Dad. 'The Beckett Arms. You know who owns it, don't you?'

'No.'

'Isobel's uncle. You'll never guess what he's called.'

I shrugged.

'Donald,' said Dad. 'Or . . . *The Don* to his mates!' He was laughing so hard, tears were rolling down his cheeks.

I ignored him and turned to my sister. 'What d'you get a job there for? Doing what?'

'Just the usual,' said Dad. 'Extortion, money laundering and the odd contract hit!'

'You won't think it's funny when you wake up and find a sheep's head in your bed!' I told him.

Dad laughed, then frowned. 'Hang on! How do you know about that?'

'It's just a bit of waitressing,' said Meg, cutting in. 'Weekends and the odd evening.' She shrugged. 'It's not like I've got a social life to interrupt—besides, I need the money. Where else am I going to find a job around here?'

'Yeah, well . . . don't say I didn't warn you.'

Dad put a hand on my shoulder and in the rasping voice of Don Corleone, said: 'Your loyalty to the family touches my heart.' Then he stood up. 'Now, what happened to those Cornettos?'

TWELVE

THE THREE SECOND RULE

'Frankenstein's monster or Friday the Thirteenth?' Dad held the masks aloft.

'I'm not going.'

When Meg mentioned that the Beckett Arms was holding a Hallowe'en bonfire at the weekend, Mum had decided it would be the perfect opportunity to integrate ourselves into the local community. Aside from my obvious reasons for not wanting to go anywhere near the place, I'd discovered it was a costume party.

'Seriously. I'd rather eat my own toe cheese.'

'You don't fancy it then.' Dad looked genuinely surprised. He'd embraced the whole dressing-up thing with disturbing enthusiasm. As we talked, he was standing there in an old boiler suit splattered with fake blood, dribbling red paint onto the blade of a chainsaw.

'It's fine. I'll stay here.' A whole evening with the house to myself—hours of uninterrupted *SlamShowdown* and Dead Frank on full blast. I couldn't wait.

'You're coming,' said Mum, thrusting my coat at me.

'You mean I don't even get a choice?'

'That's right.'

'What?' I spluttered. 'This *is* supposed to be a free country, you know—not a dictatorship! I *am* a free man!'

'Not until you're eighteen you're not, mate. Until then, you're ours.' Dad winked at me.

The Frankenstein's monster mask stank of rubber and the eyeholes were in the wrong place. I took it off and stuffed the thing into my coat pocket. It was my one concession to dressing-up, but Mum and Dad couldn't force me to actually wear it. I was still coming to terms with being press-ganged into an evening of excruciating boredom and potential embarrassment with my parents—both of whom were dressed like idiots. OK, I'll admit that Mum's skeleton catsuit and skull face paint did actually look quite good—but seriously, G, she wasn't eight years old any more.

As we approached the village, the Beckett Arms floated into view, shimmering with noise and colour against the darkness of the hillside. I was moderately impressed by the effort they'd made to spook the place up. Strings of pumpkin lanterns swayed in the wind, while a layer of dry ice rolled across the car park like fog. It would have been really creepy if Michael Jackson's 'Thriller' hadn't been blasting out over everything.

The bonfire was in the field behind. You could see the flames from the road, spitting sparks into the air like kamikaze fireflies, swirling in the smoke until their brief, bright lives were extinguished by the cold.

'Blimey!' said Dad. 'They've really pushed the boat out for this one.'

'It's quite an event apparently,' said Mum. 'I heard people come from all over the valley.'

I didn't like the sound of that. I'd assumed it would be a sad little local gathering—a bunch of old people in witch's hats sitting around a bonfire—but the place was swarming with bodies—literally. We were surrounded by a rotting multitude of the un-dead and unholy. Everywhere I looked there were vampires, zombies, and bed-sheet ghosts. I couldn't have stood out more if I'd been naked. I grabbed the Frankenstein's monster mask from my pocket and put it on, then pulled the hood up on my parka. I just hoped nobody asked me who I was supposed to be.

A barbecue had been set up next to a large striped marquee at the side of the pub. Dad's food radar guided us in, and we found Meg standing behind a line of tables in a purple witch's hat, serving burgers and hot-dogs.

'Didn't expect to see you here,' she said, when I arrived at the front of the queue.

'They made me.'

She laughed and dropped a blackened sausage onto my paper plate. 'Have fun!'

'Yeah, right . . .'

When I looked up and saw Mum and Dad were talking to a pair of zombies by the mustard table, I decided it might be a good time to find a nice quiet spot to hide. I was three metres from the exit when a familiar shape blocked my path.

'Well, well! If it isn't my favourite southern transvestite!' Gareth had dark glasses on, even though it was pitch black outside. His hair had been back-combed into a quiff and he was wearing a large overcoat with the collar turned up. It took me a moment to work out that he was supposed to be the bloke from *Twilight*, though to be honest, G, he looked more like a fat Elvis. 'What you doing here, Kecks?'

'I've been wondering that myself,' I said, wishing I hadn't taken the mask off to eat my hot-dog. 'What about you?'

'My old man and Don are best mates,' he said, nodding towards a crowded table tucked away at the end of the marquee. 'Like family really.' That made sense. Gareth was probably being trained up to be one of Don Skinner's enforcers.

I was about to ask which one of the people at the table was the famous local mafia boss, but realized I didn't need to. All eyes were on Psycho's uncle.

He was older than I expected, tall and slim with grey slicked-back hair. When he spoke, everyone listened. He smiled when he made a joke, but never fully joined in the laughter that followed. There was something about him that reminded me of The Beast—that same quiet confidence that oozed menace.

'Who are you supposed to be anyway?' said Gareth, stepping back to look me up and down.

'Um . . . I didn't know it was fancy dress.'

He frowned. 'Don't let Don see you like that. He thinks it's disrespectful when people don't dress up!'

I nodded and edged past him towards the exit. 'Right, well, I'll see you later. Cool Elvis outfit by the way.'

'Elvis?' said Gareth, but I was already out of the tent, laughing into my hot-dog.

The field was full of people, their bodies silhouetted by the glare from the flames. I felt the heat as I approached and could hear the crack and spit of burning wood. I walked up the slope until the bonfire was between me and the pub. There was nobody else this far up and it was cold away from the fire, but the darkness provided good cover.

I was staring into the flames, munching my hot-dog, when something nudged my paper plate. I looked down and found myself gazing into the eyes of The Beast. I swore—took a step backwards and tripped. When I looked up, Psycho Skinner was once again standing over me. I noticed that she wasn't in fancy dress either.

'Hope you didn't want that,' she said.

I followed the direction of her eyes and saw the dog gulping down the remains of my sausage.

'I did actually!' I said, scrambling to my feet.

Psycho smirked. 'Shouldn't have dropped it then.'

'I didn't drop it. Your dog . . .'

'My dog, what?' The Beast ambled over and stood obediently at her side, licking slivers of fried onion from its lips. They were both staring at me. The girl and the dog. I swear I saw flames, G. Little flickering fires deep in their sockets, like peeking through a keyhole into hell. Thinking about it now, I suppose it could just have been the reflection of the bonfire, but all the same . . .

'You shouldn't creep up on people like that,' I said. 'The dog made me jump.'

If Psycho hadn't laughed, I probably would have just walked away. But she did, so I said:

'I've been meaning to ask. What is it you're up to, exactly?'

She frowned. 'Just bringing my dog out for a leak, if you really want to know.'

'No! I mean, why are you pretending to help my mum?'

For a moment Psycho looked confused. Then she laughed again. 'You're serious aren't you? Bloody hell!' She shook her head. 'I'm helping your mum because she asked me. Because I like helping her. You got a problem with that—*Marcus*?'

'Yeah, I have actually. Especially as it's your fault she needs help in the first place!'

'You what? How d'you work that one out?'

'If you hadn't set that *thing* on me,' I pointed at The Beast, 'I wouldn't have had to climb a tree. And if I hadn't been up the tree, I couldn't have fallen out of it into the road. If I hadn't been in the road, Mum wouldn't have had to crash the car to not run me over.' I stopped, realizing I'd already said too much.

Psycho frowned. 'You know what? I don't understand a word of what you just said.' She stared at me, then clicked her tongue at The Beast. 'Come on, Lucky, let's leave the strange boy alone.'

'I'm not the one who's strange!' I shouted after them. She either didn't hear, or didn't care.

'I dunno,' said a voice. 'Talking to yourself. That's a bit strange.' When I turned around Gareth was walking towards me, the firelight reflecting off the bottle of lager he was holding. 'And what did you mean, *Elvis*?'

Shit!

Dad was still inside the marquee. I had the feeling he might have been there all night.

'What happened to you?' he said, brushing at the mud on my coat.

'I slipped.'

'Slipped? Looks like you've been mud wrestling.'

'I kind of slipped and . . . rolled a bit.' I shrugged. 'Where's Mum? Can we go yet?'

He pointed to where Mum was talking animatedly to a figure in a black hooded cloak, holding a very realistic looking scythe.

'Who's the Grim Reaper?'

Dad chuckled. 'That's Isobel's dad. I reckon she's getting us connected!'

'OK, but when she's finished talking, can we just go? Seriously, my brain cells are dying from sheer boredom!'

He laughed. 'Hey, what did you think of the hot-dog, then?'

'I dropped the last bit.'

'Dropped it!' His eyes widened. 'Where? Couldn't you have picked it up? Three second rule!'

I frowned. I wasn't sure the three second rule counted if your sausage was halfway down a dog's throat before the time was up.

'D'you fancy another one?'

'I just want to go, Dad.'

'Come on, one last hot-dog and then I'll talk to your mum. But this time you've got to try the chilli pepper mustard. Talk about killing off brain cells!' He whistled.

I needed some Dead Frank.

My mobile was in my coat pocket. I reached for it, debating whether the occasion called for the raw energy of *Spilt Milk*, or the more experimental, but just as good *No use crying over* . . . Except, my phone wasn't there.

I tried my jeans, my hoodie, and then my coat again, taking everything out just to be sure.

A sick feeling crawled into my gut.

My mobile was gone. It must have fallen out when I fell over—when Psycho's dog jumped me. Or it could have been when Gareth expressed his disappointment at being called Elvis. Either way, it had to be somewhere on the field.

'Dad! Gotta go!' I ran out of the marquee, dodging through the crowd, and sprinted up the hill to the darkness where I'd met Psycho and then Gareth. I crouched down, running my hands over the muddy grass. After a few minutes I found my paper plate—a few onions and a smear of tomato sauce still stuck to it, but no phone. I kept looking, widening the search, but it was hopeless—too dark and too much field.

Maybe someone had picked it up?

When I got back, Dad was juggling two hot-dogs. He tried to hand one to me, but I shook my head. 'Can I borrow your phone?'

I found my name in Dad's contacts list and pressed *call*, praying for someone to pick up—but after three rings, my voicemail kicked in. I was almost too disappointed to leave a message.

'Somebody might have handed it in,' said Dad. 'I'll go and check at the bar.'

He came back ten minutes later shaking his head.

My whole life was on that phone.

Email, text, messenger—all gone.

Without it, the only way to contact anyone back home would be to borrow Mum's laptop and hope the string-and-yoghurt-pots internet connection on Scar Hill would last long enough to send a message.

Then there was the video of Frog trying to jump the gate into Tuna's back garden and ending up in the wheelie-bin. We were going to send that in to *Video Funnies*, the TV programme where they pay you money for clips of people doing stupid things. Now it was gone.

Worst of all—and it made me feel sick just thinking about it—was the music I'd lost. Half the stuff on my phone had come from Jack's brother Richie. I'd always meant to copy it onto my laptop, but somehow never got round to it.

All my Dead Frank, Cigarette UFO, and Prayer for Halo—gone.

I hadn't just lost a phone. I'd lost everything.

THIRTEEN

'WISH ME LUCK'

I couldn't remember the last time I'd been up so early on a weekend, G. The field behind the Beckett Arms was silver with frost, apart from the dark scar left by the bonfire. A rich, woody dampness hung on the icy wind, and when I walked over and stood for a moment at the edge of the blackened circle, I could see tails of smoke and feel the heat still radiating from within.

After a fruitless five minutes scouring the spot where I'd encountered Psycho and Gareth, I was forced to accept that I was going to have to do a systematic search of the entire area.

There were all sorts of things on the ground: cigarette butts, napkins, paper plates, crisp packets, bread rolls, bottles—coins even. I'd found sixty pence by the time I got to the hedge, but no phone.

I was beginning the next sweep when I saw someone walking towards me across the field. It took a few seconds to register that it was Don Skinner himself—mainly because of what he was wearing. There was something slightly disturbing about the red silk dressing gown, not to mention the fact that I could see a lot more of his skinny old man legs than I wanted to.

Apparently, in the moment before you die, your entire life flashes in front of your eyes. How anybody knows this, I'm not sure, but as I waited for Don Skinner to reach me, all the violent bits from *The Godfather* played in my head on fast forward.

'You must be Megan's brother,' he said, without a trace of a rasp in his voice. 'Oz, isn't it?' I was both surprised and unnerved that he knew my name.

I nodded.

'She said you'd lost your phone. I take it that's why you're here.'

I managed to croak in the affirmative, and tried not to stare at the deep scar running down the side of his face. I was amazed how he could stand there, in what was, let's face it, a seriously dodgy dressing gown, and still make me feel like *I* was the one who'd been caught half-dressed.

'Want to earn yourself a bit of money while you're here?'

I wasn't ready for that.

'Um . . . ' What was he going to ask me to do? What would happen if I refused?

'I just thought if you're going to be scouring every blade of grass looking for your phone, you might as well pick up the rubbish while you're at it.' Don Skinner looked past me over the field. 'I'll pay you.' His eyes snapped back and locked onto mine. 'How does ten quid sound?' He phrased it like a question—but I could tell it wasn't.

Ten quid was rapidly sounding like a measly amount for two hours picking litter and freezing my arse off. The lower part of my back ached from bending over, and I'd lost all feeling in my toes and fingers. I'd almost reached the line of trees at the top of the field and still hadn't found the phone. It was pointless searching any further.

Don Skinner was dressed when I returned to the pub, and strangely enough looked less menacing in normal clothes. 'Any luck?' he asked.

I shook my head.

'Was it expensive?'

I shrugged. 'It's got all my music on . . . and this really funny video of my mate falling into a wheelie-bin . . . ' I stopped. What was I doing telling Don Skinner about Frog and the wheelie-bin?

But he laughed. 'You should have sent that in to the telly. How much is it they pay these days?'

'Two hundred . . . or something.'

'Could have bought a new phone with that!'

'Yeah . . . I suppose I could.' I wondered if he was deliberately trying to make me feel bad.

I followed him down a narrow corridor that smelt of stale beer and chips, into a tiny office piled high with boxes. It was a far cry from Don Corleone's luxurious study in *The Godfather*. There was barely enough room for both of us to squeeze inside. I noticed an ancient computer monitor squatting on one corner of the desk, next to a rash of dirty coffee mugs and an overflowing ashtray. Then I saw the money—piles of the stuff—like a model of the New York skyline made from skyscrapers of ten and twenty pound notes.

'That's a lot of cash!' I said, before I could stop myself.

Don grunted. 'We always do well when we put a special night on, so I suppose it's worth the extra effort.'

Especially when it's not you who has to clean up, I thought. Though this time, thankfully, the words stayed in my head.

Two minutes later I was crossing the car park pushing a ten pound note into the pocket of my jeans. A tenner! No wonder Skinner was loaded. But then, a whole building's worth of notes wouldn't have made up for everything I'd lost. The entire morning had been a waste of time. Now I had a twenty minute walk up the hill in the freezing wind to look forward to and no Dead Frank to blot out the pain.

I noticed the car parked at the bus stop the moment I crossed the road. It appeared to have been put together from parts of at least three different vehicles. The badge on the back suggested it had once been a silver Ford Fiesta. It now had one red door and one blue. The front wing was metallic green and the bonnet bright yellow. As I drew level, the red door swung open and a tall skinny kid got out.

'This is . . . Slowleigh, right?' he said, pushing the blond fringe out of his eyes and frowning at a piece of paper. His accent and pronunciation were unmistakably southern.

I nodded. 'Afraid so.'

'I'm looking for . . . *Scar Hill Lane* . . . d'you know it?'

'I live that way. You can give me a lift.'

'Yeah? Thanks, mate.'

I walked round to the passenger side of the car and opened the blue door. The seat was covered in takeaway cartons, chocolate wrappers, and CDs.

'Sorry about the mess,' he said, tossing the rubbish into the back. 'Jump in.'

'Hang on.' I paused, my hand on the door. 'What if you're like, a pervert or something?' He looked surprised. 'I mean, well . . . you could be anyone, couldn't you?'

'I'm Kris,' he said, offering his hand. 'Kris-with-a-K.'

Somehow, G, I managed to keep my face straight as we shook hands and I sat down.

'So . . . did you build this car yourself?' I tried to sound normal, like I was just making conversation.

'I bought it off a mate,' he said, turning the ignition. The car whined but didn't start.

'Are you sure he put an engine in?'

Kris glanced at me and for a second he looked hurt, then he laughed. 'I know—it looks like a pile of junk, but it's all I could afford. And it does go . . . usually. Just sometimes needs a bit of coaxing.' He stamped his foot on the accelerator a few times, then turned the key again. Nothing.

'So . . . what brings you to Slowleigh, Kris?'

His face clouded. 'Um . . . just visiting someone. A friend.'

'What's her name?'

He squinted at me. 'How d'you know it's a girl. I never said.'

'Lucky guess?' *Careful*, Oz.

Kris sighed and sat back in his seat. 'You're right though. It is a girl.'

'Girl . . . friend?'

'Sort of.'

'She expecting you? Or is this a surprise visit?'

'You ask a lot of questions, don't you?' He reached into his jacket. 'D'you mind waiting five minutes while I have a fag? Give the car a chance to dry out. I think it might be flooded.' I watched as Kris took out cigarette papers and a pouch.

So Meg didn't know he was coming. I wondered if I should own up about who I was. I mean, did he know about the baby? Should *I* tell him? Then again, maybe it would be better to keep quiet, at least until I found out how much he knew.

'She'll be pleased to see you then?' I said.

Kris snorted, rolling the paper and tobacco into a thin tube and lifting it to his lips. 'Dunno about that.'

'Why? What did you do?'

He frowned.

'I mean, people only end up here if they've done something to deserve it.'

'So what did *you* do?' said Kris, lighting his cigarette.

'Ah, well, by rights, I shouldn't be here.'

'Yeah?'

'You see before you an innocent man,' I said, raising my palms.

'Nobody's innocent,' said Kris.

'So what *did* you do?'

He took a long drag on the cigarette, then exhaled through his nose in a thin grey stream. 'She's pregnant.'

'Pregnant!' I tried my best to sound suitably surprised. 'Really? Wow!'

He frowned. 'I *think* so. I only found out last night. One of her mates told me.' Kris sounded angry, but then my sister had that effect on people. 'I didn't know what to do. I tried ringing but she didn't answer.'

Meg would have been at the Hallowe'en bonfire, she wouldn't have heard her phone. Or perhaps she was screening her calls.

'I sat up all night,' said Kris, 'trying to think what to do. I had to find out if it was true. So I drove here. I've been on the road since four o'clock this morning.' He took another drag on the roll-up and gave a half-hearted laugh. 'It's probably a load of rubbish. I've probably driven all this way for nothing, yeah?'

I wondered again if I should say something, prepare him for the shock of what was waiting at the top of Scar Hill.

But once he knew, there was no un-knowing.

I decided to let Kris enjoy his last few minutes of ignorant bliss.

'Right!' He leaned forward and clutched the steering wheel. 'Wish me luck.'

I wasn't sure if he meant with starting the car, or the rest of his life.

'Are you sure this is a real road?' said Kris, gripping the steering wheel with both hands.

'Yeah, keep going, it's not far now.'

'Where d'you live, anyway? Tell me where you want dropping off.'

'The farm's fine.' I was beginning to wish I'd told him the truth, but it was too late now, I could see the house up ahead. 'That's it,' I told Kris. 'Take the next right . . . watch out for the wall.'

The car bumped along the track leading to the yard. 'Is this definitely the right place?' Kris leant forward to peer through the windscreen. 'It looks like something out of a horror film.'

'Could well be,' I muttered, imagining the reception he might be about to receive.

Kris parked by the gate and switched off the engine. 'Right. S'pose I better get this over with.'

'Good luck.'

He nodded. 'Thanks. You sure you're OK from here?'

'Yeah, this is perfect.'

By the time Kris had trudged all the way round the building to the front door, I'd gone in the back way to the kitchen. Fortunately Mum was halfway down the stairs when he knocked. I strained to hear the conversation.

'Kris!' To say Mum sounded surprised was an understatement. If she'd opened the door to find Guy Fawkes himself standing there, she couldn't have been any more astonished. 'What a lovely surprise,' she said, and I had to admit, she hid it well.

I heard Kris ask about her arm, and then realized they were coming towards the kitchen. It was too late to hide.

'That's quite a drive,' Mum was saying. 'Megan didn't mention you were coming.'

'Um . . . she doesn't know. I . . . ' Kris stopped, his eyes boggling as he spotted me.

'This is Marcus, Megan's brother,' said Mum. 'Marcus, this is . . . '

'Kris-with-a-K! Fancy seeing you here!'

Strangely enough, Kris didn't look that delighted to see me again.

Mum frowned. 'I didn't think you two had met.'

'Oh, we go way back.'

I could feel Mum watching us, trying to work out what was going on. 'Marcus, why don't you make Kris a cup of tea, while I go and see if your sister's awake.'

'No need,' I said, nodding towards the doorway.

Meg was standing there, dressed in her saggy grey pyjamas and Dr Martens, hair sticking up in all directions. *She* wasn't smiling either.

FOURTEEN

SWIMMING TO THE MOON

It was like waiting for a bomb to go off. Meg looked terrified and couldn't get Kris out of the house fast enough. She ran upstairs and got dressed, then claimed they were going for a walk—*to see the sights*. There *were* no sights and Meg hated walks. She just wanted to get outside, so that when she finally told Kris the good news, any ensuing screams would be swallowed by the wind.

To be honest, G, it was a bit of a let down. Like saving the biggest firework until last on bonfire night. It's called something scary like *The Annihilator* and has instructions to stand at least five miles away, preferably in an adjacent country. You're holding your breath, tensing every muscle, waiting for some incredible ball-shrinking explosion. Except, when it finally goes off, all you get is coloured smoke and a farty pop that doesn't even wake the cat.

They were gone for less than an hour, but when Meg and Kris trooped back in, I knew she'd told him. Kris had a distracted look in his eyes, as though he could see his old life slipping away and a new one descending in its place. I recognized that look, G, because I knew exactly how he felt.

I'd been putting off firing up my laptop to find out exactly what music I'd lost on my phone. Deep down I knew that the files I'd got from Jack's brother had never been copied onto the computer, but it still hurt seeing the truth spelt out on screen. When my search for 'Dead Frank' returned the message *No Files Found* I felt like crying. It might not sound like much but Dead Frank had kept me going these past weeks. I seriously didn't know what I would do without them.

My steam-driven laptop was so old it refused to go online any more, so I borrowed Mum's and sent a message to Jack. With our rubbish connection there was no way I'd be able to download the albums again myself, so I asked him to burn me a disc of all the important stuff I'd lost. Jack would understand exactly how serious the situation was, and with any luck I'd get a parcel by the end of the week. Even so, the next few days were going to be tough, G.

When I saw The Beast mooching around the yard, cocking his leg up our wall like he owned the place, I knew Psycho was in the studio. It had occurred to me that there was a chance she'd seen me drop the phone and picked it up.

I had to find out. I was aware that our exchange the previous evening hadn't gone particularly well. If I wanted Psycho's co-operation, I was going to have to be nice to her. That walk to the barn was one of the hardest journeys of my life, G.

Stepping into Mum's studio felt like entering an alternative reality. The air was heavy with the smell of coffee and acetone, the steady hiss of the calor gas heaters and the flickering blue flame of the blow torch. Even the lamps, suspended on a web of wires, had a pioneering, new world feel—except this was a land populated by giant robotic insects.

As I squeezed through the heavy wooden door, I could see that Mum was working on something new. There was a framework of twisted pipes in the centre of the barn, as though someone had started putting up a tent, then got angry and bent all the poles out of shape.

Psycho was kneeling on the floor with her back to me, hammering the life out of a sheet of twisted metal. The noise was immense, clattering off the walls and filling the air with swirling dust and flakes of paint. There was something deeply disturbing, but horribly fascinating, about the level of violence she was bringing down on the thing.

Psycho must have sensed me watching because she stopped and her head snapped round in my direction. She was wearing goggles and ear-defenders, and at that moment looked a lot like an insect herself. I opened my mouth to speak, but before any words came out she was on her feet, hurtling towards me with the hammer raised above her head.

I had just enough time to think: *what?* and *seriously?* before being slammed back against the wall. I closed my eyes and waited for the skull shattering explosion of pain. When it didn't arrive, I opened them again and found Psycho standing in front of me, shaking with laughter.

'What did you do that for?' I screamed.

'You shouldn't creep up on people like that,' she said, in a whiny voice. 'You made me jump.'

I bit down on the words throwing themselves at my teeth to get out, and reminded myself to be nice.

Psycho was still smirking. 'Was there something you wanted?' she said, making it sound like it was *her* barn we were standing in. 'Your mum's gone inside.'

'I know. I need to talk to you.'

'Me? I'm honoured.'

'Last night. When your dog . . . ' I sighed. 'When I *slipped* over—I dropped my phone.'

'So?'

'I thought you might have picked it up.'

'Oh, so I'm a thief as well now am I?'

'No. That's not what I meant . . . '

She scowled. 'You don't learn, do you?'

'I just wondered if you'd seen it. I wasn't accusing you of anything.'

'Good job,' said Psycho, passing the hammer from one hand to the other.

I sighed. 'Look, did you see my phone, or not?'

She stared at me for a long time, then let out a snort. 'Not.'

'Right.' There wasn't a lot to say after that.

I wasn't impressed to find Dad unfolding an antique camp bed in my room.

'What's going on?'

'Kris is staying for a few days,' he said. 'I don't know how that old banger of his made it all the way up here, but I think the effort might have killed it.'

'But why are you putting that in here?'

'I was hoping you'd let Kris have your bed.'

'Which means I have to sleep on that?'

'It's only for a couple of nights,' he said, unrolling a sleeping bag and giving it a sniff.

'Why can't he go in Meg's room?'

Dad looked suddenly uncomfortable. He coughed. 'Well . . . there's more space up here.'

Yeah, right.

When I heard Kris coming up the stairs later that evening, I pretended to be asleep. All day it had been obvious he was still in a mood with me, and I didn't feel like a lecture.

I lay there with my eyes screwed shut, listening to him moving around. When he finally got into bed, I waited a few more minutes before rolling over.

'If you want to pretend you're asleep,' he said, 'don't hold your breath.' Kris stared at me from across the attic, the moonlight casting deep shadows across his face. 'Why didn't you tell me who you were?'

'I didn't realize it was you at first,' I said. 'And then, well . . . If you'd known who I was, you would have started asking me about the baby. What was I supposed to do? Meg would have gone mental if I'd told you.'

I waited, but he didn't say anything.

'So now you know, d'you feel better?'

Kris rolled onto his back and sighed at the ceiling. 'I dunno. I suppose.'

'What you going to do? Have you told Mum and Dad?'

He shook his head. 'Meg doesn't want to . . . not yet.'

'Don't you think they're going to get suspicious though? I mean, especially now you're here and everything.'

'They think I just came up so I could get back with Meg.'

I could imagine Dad lapping that up, he was soft as anything. I'd caught him crying over films more than once. Mum was so focused on her exhibition I doubted she would have given it much thought. It wouldn't even occur to them that their superhero darling daughter might be up the duff!

'So what *are* you going to do?' I said.

Kris turned his face towards me. 'Look . . . I'm knackered, mate. It's been a really long day. Can we talk about this in the morning?' He rolled over and within minutes I could hear him snoring.

Perfect! While Kris lay drooling onto my pillow, I was wide awake, trying to achieve the impossible and get comfortable on the Cramp Bed. The mattress was the thickness of a tissue, and the sleeping bag kept unzipping itself and sliding onto the floor. Every time I moved, some sharp piece of metal jabbed me in the back. It was like trying to sleep on a bag of spanners. I couldn't even listen to any music without my phone.

With nothing to distract it, my brain was throwing out random thoughts. I found myself thinking about Meg in her room on the floor below—how she was pregnant and everything. That made me think about you, G—this tiny Foam Shrimp Alien all curled up inside her.

Hey, G—you awake?

The moment I thought it, I felt like an idiot. But then this voice answered—just appeared in my head, like a new text message arriving.

No.

That's what you said. Which I thought was quite funny, so I answered.

Me, neither. What you doing?

I'm a baby! I'm not even born yet. What do you think I'm doing?

Good point. Must get boring in there.

Nah, it's OK. Nice and warm. It's a bit like being in the bath, only the water never goes cold.

Wow! You've been in there for weeks. You must be pretty wrinkly by now.

Like a prune. I think. I don't know. I'm not sure what a prune is, that just came into my head. My skin's all big and baggy though. I think it's the wrong size.

Maybe you'll grow into it.

Yeah, probably. What you doing?

Not sleeping. Listening to your dad snoring.

My dad! He's with you! What's he like?

Dunno, really. I only met him today. Seems all right. He drove all the way up here to find out about you.

For me? That must mean he's OK.

Yeah. I suppose so.

I shook my head. Since when did I start having imaginary conversations with my sister's unborn baby? What was happening to me? There must be something in the water round here. I was sure I'd heard Meg going on about some town near a nuclear power station where all the babies had been born with two heads or six fingers. Maybe the whole valley was infected. It would certainly explain a few things.

I pulled the sleeping bag up and re-arranged my pillow in a vain attempt to get comfortable. I might as well have tried swimming to the moon.

FIFTEEN

'NOW THAT'S WHAT *I* CALL A DISASTER'

Thanks to the Cramp Bed and not having the alarm on my phone to wake me up, I overslept and was too late to catch the bus. Dad dropped me off when he took Mum to work, but I still missed registration and the start of first period.

It was break time before I saw Ryan crossing the quad towards the field. I set off after him, anticipating the look on his face when I told him I'd been paid to *do a job* for Don Skinner. But where the hell was he going?

Like most kids, Ryan followed a regular daily routine. Break times were spent either in the library or on the steps by the hall—areas beyond the radar-range of Gareth and his mates. So this was a deviation.

I watched Ryan disappear around the corner of the science block, but when I reached it there was no sign of him. The path was a dead end, leading to a storage area for the recycling skips. I was about to turn around when I heard a noise—a scuffle of feet and the sound of a bag landing on concrete. I walked along the line of bins and found Ryan slouched against the wall at the far end.

'What you doing here?'

He looked up briefly, but didn't answer.

I dropped my rucksack and sat down next to him. 'Hey, guess who I did a job for on Sunday?'

Ryan's shoulders barely moved.

'Don Skinner!'

I waited for Ryan to leap to his feet in wide-eyed amazement; to start waving his arms about and hyperventilating.

He just sat there.

'Did you hear what I said?'

Ryan nodded, but didn't look up.

'You should have seen the piles of cash in his office!' I said. 'And he was like . . .' I put on a rasping Don Corleone voice. 'I want you to do a job for me.' I laughed. 'I nearly dropped my load! I thought he was going to ask me to do a hit or something!'

Ryan turned his face towards me.

'And you know that stupid Hallowe'en party I told you about? I lost my phone! That's why I was at the pub—trying to find it, but it's gone! It's a complete disaster!'

'You think losing your phone is a complete disaster?' He spoke so quietly, I wasn't sure if he was talking to me, or himself.

'Well . . . yeah! It had all my music on. All my Dead Frank. Gone!'

I expected a reaction, but Ryan didn't say anything. In fact I was beginning to wonder if there was something seriously wrong, when he suddenly growled and slammed a fist against his leg. 'I don't understand how they got hold of it,' he said, almost shouting. 'It doesn't make any sense!'

'What are you on about?'

He pulled out his mobile and jabbed at the keys like he was trying to inflict pain on the phone, then virtually threw it at me. 'This! It's gone round the whole school. You must be the only one who hasn't seen it!'

'I told you, I lost my . . .' I stopped when I saw the image on the screen. It was a picture of Ryan dressed as a hobbit, with his little sword and his hairy feet socks . . . and it was horribly familiar.

I felt my face flush. 'Where d'you get this?'

'Someone sent it to me. It's going round the whole school.'

I swore and Ryan nodded. 'Yeah, now that's what *I* call a disaster!'

I guessed from the fact that Ryan was still talking to me, that he hadn't realized the photo was one from his own bedroom wall.

He snatched the phone back and threw it into his bag. 'Apparently, there's more on the internet. I haven't seen them yet—just this one.'

'What?' I stared at him.

'The thing is,' said Ryan. 'That photo must have been taken at *Fight Camp* last summer, but I didn't think anybody from school was there.'

'What's *Fight Camp*?'

Ryan looked down and kicked at the ground. 'We camp out in the woods and do re-enactments . . . of battles from fantasy books. Last year was the *Ambush in Ithilien* from *Lord of the Rings*.'

'Right,' I said, only half listening. The rest of my brain was busy trying to work out the implications of what I had just learned.

A small part—no, I won't lie to you, G—a large part of me was struggling to keep the grin off my face, at the knowledge that my phone was still intact. On the other hand, the fact that whoever picked it up had found the pictures of Ryan and gone to the trouble of posting them on the internet, did not bode well. It suggested that the person in question was probably not your average well-meaning citizen, and quite possibly didn't like me very much.

Had I decided to draw up a list of suspects matching those criteria, it would have required a large sheet of paper. But there was no need. I knew who had it. She'd had the opportunity and the motive. The fact that Psycho Skinner had denied it to my face meant nothing.

Then I started to wonder what other treats she might have in store—and didn't feel quite so much like grinning. Add to that, the fact that once Ryan saw the rest of the photos, he would realize it was me who had taken them.

I had the horrible feeling that the weekend's disasters were just the start. The Wheel of Destiny was picking up speed, G, and I didn't have a clue how I was going to slow it down.

Kris-with-a-K was in my room when I got home.

'Sorry,' he said. 'I was just changing my T-shirt. I can come back later.'

'It's OK.'

'I should be out your way soon anyway,' he said, rooting through his bag.

'Is the car fixed?'

'Not yet, but your dad's having a look at it for me. We'll go when it's done.'

'We?'

Kris looked up. 'Yeah. Meg's coming with me.'

I let my rucksack fall to the floor.

'I've got a place in Parkview with a couple of mates, but there's room for one—well, two more.' Kris gave a crooked smile. 'I mean, it's my baby—my responsibility, right?'

I sat down on the Cramp Bed.

Kris peeled off his shirt and gave his armpits a sniff. 'We've been talking loads since I got here and . . . we've decided that's what we want to do. I mean, like Meg says, just because we're young, doesn't mean we can't be good parents, yeah.' He was still nodding as he pulled a creased T-shirt from the bag.

I could imagine how the *talks* he'd had with Meg would have gone. I almost felt sorry for him.

'Do Mum and Dad know?'

Kris shook his head, then frowned. 'I probably shouldn't have told you either. You'd better not say anything!'

'Relax! I wouldn't dream of it.'

'What do you want, Oz? I'm busy.' Meg was getting ready to go out, I knew the signs. The air seeping from her room was heavy with perfume and the terrible music she listens to.

'We need to talk.'

'I told you, I'm busy.' Meg tried to close the door, but I blocked it with my foot. 'I'll break your foot then, I don't care!'

'OK, if you want me to shout through the door about you running away with Kris, I can do!'

My sister swore and pulled me into the room. 'Christ! What did he tell *you* for?'

I grinned. 'People tell me things. I've got an honest face.'

'You say anything to Mum and Dad, and I'll kill you. I mean it, Oz!'

'Not a very good example to set for Gonzo!'

Meg grabbed a handful of my hair. For all her sloganeering, my sister wasn't opposed to a bit of violent oppression herself.

'OK! Relax! It was a joke.' I raised my palms in surrender. 'Look, why should I say anything? I'll be happy to see you go. I can have your room.'

Meg scowled and released her grip. 'Fine. Have it. But if you don't care, why did you come down here?'

'I just wanted to check Krispy wasn't winding me up. I mean, you've got to admit, it does sound like a joke. You and Gonzo with Krispy Kris and his mates in some squat in Parkview. One big happy family.'

'It's not a squat! Anyway, it's only temporary, until we can get a place on our own.'

'So that's it. You're really going then?'

She nodded.

'What about Mum and Dad?'

'What about them? I doubt Mum will even notice I'm gone!'

'Are you going to tell them or just run away?'

'I'm not running away, Oz. I just don't see the point in having an argument. I'm going whatever they say.' She frowned and fiddled with the belt on her dressing gown. 'I'll talk to them when I've gone.'

'Oh, that's just great. Don't forget I'll still be here to cop the fallout. Thanks for that!'

She laughed and put an arm around my shoulders. 'Just see getting my room as compensation.'

'Yeah, well—just make sure you tidy up before you go. And I shouldn't leave this lying around either, it's a bit of a giveaway.' I picked up *Baby's Journey* from the floor.

Meg grunted.

'So what does Gonzo look like now?' I said, flicking through the transforming baby pictures.

Meg pointed to the right page and I read the text under the drawing. 'Hey, Gonzo! It says here that you are now officially a foe— . . . how do you say that?'

'Foetus, idiot! Keep your voice down! And don't call him that!'

'What?'

'Gonzo!'

'It's a good name.' I grinned and read aloud from the book. '*Baby is now a foetus.*' Pronounced *feet-us*, by the way, G, just so you know. '*All body parts are beginning to grow: arms, legs, eyes and main organs. Baby will almost double in size in the next three weeks.*' I laughed. 'Hey, d'you hear that, fat boy?'

Meg grabbed the book and stuffed it into the bottom of a drawer, then opened the door. 'Goodbye, Oz.'

I stood up. 'You know, your interpersonal skills could really do with some work, sis.'

'OUT!'

SIXTEEN

HOW TO MAKE FRIENDS

It started the moment Ryan got on the bus. A voice called out from the back—

'Mr Frodo, sir!'

To which somebody responded—

'I didn't know this bus stopped at The Shire!'

It was hard keeping a straight face, and I'm not proud to admit that I was relieved when Ryan didn't sit in the empty seat next to me. I tried telling myself that he was staying at the front to be further away from the jibes, but I'd caught the look he gave me. It confirmed that he'd seen the photos and worked out that I was responsible. He probably thought I'd posted them on the internet as well. Why wouldn't he?

The barrage of comments continued for the entire journey to school—a stream of references to *Lord of the Rings*, the Beatles, dressing-up and being gay. Some were actually quite funny, but the majority plain nasty. I flinched as the words flew over my head like a hail of arrows and hoped that Ryan couldn't hear them. But who was I kidding? Even the driver chuckled when someone shouted out:

'I bet he wishes *he* had a ring that would make him disappear!'

By the time I'd fought my way through the crowd getting off the bus, Ryan was halfway down the road.

'Ryan, I'm sorry!' I said, when I caught up with him. 'It wasn't me! Well . . . it was, but I didn't mean it.'

He ignored me and kept walking.

'Look, it wasn't me who put the pictures on the net. I lost my phone—remember? Someone must have found it and . . . '

He stopped suddenly and wheeled round to face me. 'But why did you take them in the first place, Oz?'

I looked at him and shrugged. 'I don't know.'

'I do,' he said. 'You took the pictures because you thought it was funny—me dressing up like that. I'm not like you, am I? With your weird shoes and your hair and your music no one's ever heard of. I'm just a joke to you, aren't I?'

'Course not! It's nothing like that.' But even as I said it, I knew that was exactly why I had taken the pictures and what I thought of him.

'You know what really gets me?' said Ryan. 'You were only in my room because I was trying to be friendly. I felt sorry for you. Everyone else was calling you names. I don't know why I bothered.'

'I'm sorry!'

'Sorry? What good's that to me?' Ryan sniffed and wiped the back of his hand across his eyes, then shook his head and walked away.

It took me a few moments to register the applause. I turned round and saw Psycho Skinner standing by the bike racks, clapping her hands.

'Impressive,' she said. 'You really know how to make friends don't you!'

'It was you!' I shouted, stalking towards her.

I was about a foot away when Psycho raised her palm. 'Really?' she said. 'You're *sure* you want to do this?'

I hesitated—not certain what I'd been planning to *do* anyway. 'Why are you doing this?' I said. 'It was just a moustache and some glasses! Can't you take a joke? I said I was sorry. You didn't have to do that to Ryan.'

When Psycho sighed and pulled a long length of chain from her bag, I took a step backwards. I felt an idiot when she crouched down and wrapped it around the frame of her bike.

'I'll say this for the last time,' she said. 'I haven't got your phone. It wasn't me. If you accuse me again, I will visit you in the night and remove your kidneys with a spoon. Understand?'

I nodded. Why she would want to use a spoon confused me a little, but the meaning was clear enough.

'Good.' Psycho pushed past and walked towards the building.

'But if it wasn't you, who was it?' I said.

She didn't answer.

Of course the prime suspect was Gareth. While Psycho's signature style was menaces with violence, Gareth was all about making people look stupid. Even though I had my answer about five seconds after voicing the question, I spent all day not doing anything about it. Don't judge me too harshly, G, but I wasn't in a hurry to repeat the whole—*what do you mean, Elvis?*—incident if I could avoid it.

Eight hours later I was sitting at the kitchen table, not doing my homework, still looking for a solution that didn't involve confronting Gareth, when Mum came in wearing her dressing gown and a towel wrapped around her hair.

'Oz, nip down to the garage and tell your dad there's a man in Thorpe Edge with a flooded kitchen, will you.' She handed me the phone. Dad still hadn't fully grasped the concept that having a mobile meant you could take it with you.

'It's raining!' I said, as the wind tossed another bucketful of water at the window.

Mum pulled a face and pointed to the phone, indicating the caller was still on the line.

I sighed, grabbed my parka and headed for the back door.

As I squelched across the yard I heard the sound of an engine coming from the small barn we use as a garage. When I pulled back the door, Dad and Kris looked up from the open bonnet of the Fiesta.

I waved the mobile in the air. 'Call-out, Dad!'

He nodded, wiping his hands on an oily rag that looked suspiciously like my old Ninja Turtle underpants, before taking the phone off me.

'You got it going then,' I said to Kris.

'Your dad's a genius!' He looked happier than I'd ever seen him. Scratch that—he looked like a man who had just been handed a ticket home.

'I'm afraid I'll have to leave you boys to it,' said Dad, picking his keys off the bench. 'It should be fine now though, Kris.'

'Thanks!'

Dad gave a thumbs-up, then stepped out into the rain. I wondered if he would have been so quick to fix the car had he known the consequences.

I turned to Kris. 'I suppose that means you'll be off then?'

He nodded. 'Probably leave in the morning.'

'Is Meg still going with you?'

'Yeah.' Kris leant into the car and switched off the engine, then picked up a stack of CDs from the passenger seat.

'Bit retro,' I said.

He shrugged. 'The iPod adaptor's broke. Anyway, I like CDs. I record my sets at the club and that.'

I remembered Kris saying he was a DJ over dinner one night. Meg had given him a look, then steered the conversation round to the graphics course he was doing at college, clearly trying to score points with Mum. I'd tried to get the subject back to music, but once Mum gets talking about art, you've got no chance.

'What sort of stuff do you play?' I asked him, preparing myself for a lame list of chart and dance rubbish.

'All sorts.' He looked up at me. 'Meg said you like your music.'

I nodded and reeled off a few of the more obscure bands I liked.

'Dead Frank were cool,' said Kris. 'Shame they split up. Have you heard Cyclops Dog?'

I was so surprised, I just stared at him—which Kris obviously took to mean *no*.

'It's Michael Death—Dead Frank's bass player and Richie Fisher from Cigarette UFO. More mellow than Dead Frank, but good stuff.' He flicked through the discs on his lap and handed one to me. 'That's got their first two EPs on. See what you think.'

'Thanks.' I was in shock. Krispy Kris-with-a-K—the lunatic in love with my sister—actually had taste—in music, if not girlfriends! Who knew?

'We're trying to get them over to play the club. My mate Rob's been in touch with the UFO's tour manager, he reckons they should be able to set something up.'

'Really?'

Kris smiled. 'I'll let you know if it happens. Put you on the guest list.'

I didn't know what to say. The thought of seeing Michael Death, the genius behind Dead Frank, was . . . too much for words.

'Have a listen and let me know what you think of the Dog anyway.' Kris walked over to the large sliding door at the side of the barn and nudged it open. I went and stood beside him. The rain was still hammering down outside. Illuminated by the light from the barn, it looked like scratches on the sky. Kris pulled out his tobacco and rolled a cigarette.

'So . . . does that mean we're related now?' I said. 'I mean, what with you being Gonzo's dad and everything?'

'Gonzo?'

'The baby. That's what Meg calls him . . . well, actually . . . that's what I call him. Meg hates it, but I reckon it's a good name. You can't keep calling it—well, *it*!'

'Gonzo? Like in the Muppets?'

'Yeah.'

He laughed. 'I quite like that.'

'So anyway, if I'm Gonzo's uncle, right. If you marry Meg, that would make us . . . ?'

'Marry?' His eyes widened. 'Did Meg say we were getting married?'

'Well . . . aren't you?'

'It's news to me, mate!'

I shrugged. 'Well, she didn't actually say you were . . . but anyway, if you did, what would that make us?'

Kris took a drag on the cigarette and frowned. 'I don't know, um . . . brothers-in-law, maybe?'

'Cool! I've always wanted a brother. There's nothing like spending your whole life with Meg to make you wish you had a brother.'

He laughed. 'She can't be that bad.'

'Can't she?'

'Go on then, give me the lowdown—so I know what to expect.'

'Are you sure you want to know?'

'How bad can it be?'

'O . . . K!' I cleared my throat. 'Well, you should know to begin with, she's never wrong, so don't bother arguing. Be prepared to find out that everything you wear, eat, drink or like to do, is actually responsible for destroying the planet and oppressing women or farmers in Brazil. Oh, and try to get rid of any cushions—she's lethal with a cushion.'

Kris frowned.

'Also, make sure you get in the bathroom first, if you want any hot water . . . and don't, whatever you do, let her near your DVDs. She never puts anything back in the right case. Other than that, she's mostly OK.'

He laughed. 'That's quite a list! Thanks for the heads-up!'

'You're welcome. Just want to make sure you know what you're letting yourself in for.'

'Better late than never, I suppose.' He looked at me and winked.

'Yeah . . . look, sorry about that.'

'It's OK. I forgive you, Oz.'

I watched the smoke from Kris's cigarette disappear into the rain.

'What would you have done?' I said. 'If I'd told you about the baby. Would you have still driven up here?

Or would you have kicked me out and gone back to Hardacre?'

'I'm not sure the car would have made it back,' he said, grinning.

I laughed and for a few minutes we just watched the rain and listened to the wind shake the trees. I thought about all those scared looking blokes from the birth pages of the baby book and just couldn't picture Kris among them.

'Where did you say your club was?'

'Frisco's in town. By the bus station.'

'Must be good being a DJ.'

'I always wanted to be in a band. Trouble is, I can't play anything and I can't sing.' He laughed. 'But I like playing other people's records. It's just good being involved in music, you know—putting bands on and stuff. I'd like to produce one day, maybe.' He shrugged. 'I guess I'll have to see how it goes.'

Kris took a final drag on the cigarette and flicked it into the night.

'I suppose we'd better go inside.'

SEVENTEEN

'DID I MISS SOMETHING?'

I woke up to find Meg leaning over me, her face uncomfortably close to mine.

'Where's Kris?' she hissed.

'What?' My eyes felt heavy. I could hear the wind outside lashing rain against the skylight, but the square of glass in the roof was black. 'What time is it?'

'Where's he gone?'

'Who?'

'Kris, you idiot!'

I pointed blindly across the room. 'In bed! It's the middle of the night!'

Meg grabbed my shoulders and forced me into a sitting position. I blinked and tried to focus on the bed opposite. It was empty.

'Hang on! Aren't you two supposed to be running away this morning?' I yawned. 'He's probably in the barn, getting the car ready.'

'Oh, I hadn't thought of that, silly me!' Meg scowled. 'I checked. The car's gone!'

'What?'

She sat back and swore. 'He's gone, Oz! Left without me!'

'But last night . . . he said he was taking you with him.'

'Yes, he mentioned you two had quite a chat. What did you say, Oz?'

'Me?'

'Yes, you! What did you do this time?'

'Nothing! We just talked about bands . . . and stuff.'

Stuff. Such as a list of reasons why living with Meg would be a bad idea.

But that had been a joke. It wasn't supposed to make Kris run off without her.

'Have you phoned him?'

'He's not answering. Big surprise.'

'What are you going to do?'

'There's not much I can do, is there.' Meg stood up, swore a few more times, then went down the steps.

I stared across the attic at the empty bed, trying to remember the details of the conversation I'd had with Kris. By the time the patch of sky above my head had paled from black to grey, I was convinced he'd left her behind because of me.

When I went down for breakfast, I was almost surprised to see my sister sitting at the table dressed for college. Of course, Mum and Dad didn't know she was supposed to have been halfway down the motorway by then, but they still thought it was odd that Kris had left so early and without saying goodbye.

'What time did he leave?' said Dad, stirring sugar into his mug.

'Early. He wanted to miss the traffic.' Meg's face was set and I couldn't tell if the tightness in her voice was anger or if she was trying not to cry.

'Did he have some breakfast before he went?'

'I don't know, Dad! Does it matter?'

'He must have left very early,' Mum said. 'I was up at six.'

'I just told you he left early! Christ!' Meg stood up so fast her chair fell over, but she didn't stop to pick it up. We heard her stamp upstairs and then her bedroom door slammed, sending a shower of dust down from the exposed ceiling.

'You think they had an argument or something?' said Dad, picking the bits out of his tea and righting the chair. 'Kris didn't say anything to you did he, Oz?'

'Me?' I felt my cheeks flush. 'Why would he talk to me?'

'Well . . . you *were* sharing a room. I just wondered if he'd mentioned leaving. Did he say goodbye or anything?'

'Oh, right . . . um, no—not that I remember.'

Kris *had* said goodbye, though—and shaken my hand. But the last thing he'd said to me before switching off the light had been, 'Wish me luck, Oz.'

To which I had laughed and replied, 'You'll need it!'

There's a boss level in *SlamShowdown* where you have to fight this creature called Gargantua. It's three times the size of all the other players. Getting near enough to land a hit is almost impossible, let alone inflict any damage. Even your best strike combo won't touch it—I mean, you might as well try to knock down a brick wall with a conker. I was stuck for weeks, unable to get past, until I realized I was approaching it all from the wrong angle.

I'd been trying all afternoon, getting to the point where I was ready to hurl the console through the window. On my last life, I didn't touch the controller, just sat back and watched as Gargantua beat its chest, roared, and slammed its armoured fists into the ground. I thought my character would be crushed in seconds—the monster was smashing the arena up all around me, but I hadn't been touched. Then, all of a sudden, Gargantua seemed to get bored. It stopped roaring and sat down, and then incredibly, it fell asleep! The thing was just lying there snoring, which is when I noticed the grenade belt it was wearing. I sneaked up, pulled the pins and ran. You should have seen the mess!

The point is, G, when you're up against someone like Gareth, there's no point trying to match them for muscle—you have to use brains.

And people say you can't learn anything from playing computer games.

The whole thing had seemed a lot more plausible when I dreamt it up in the attic, than it did as I walked across the quad to where Gareth was hassling some Year Seven kid. But it was too late to turn back.

'Hey, Kecks!' said Gareth. 'Where's your little hobbit? Or has he turned invisible?' He laughed and swiped at the air next to me. The Year Seven took the opportunity to scarper.

'I want my phone back,' I said, thinking the direct approach was best—before I lost my nerve.

Gareth pulled what I imagine he thought was an expression of innocence. It looked like he'd just farted and followed through.

'Look, I know it was you. Just give me the phone back and I won't say anything to the police.'

'You what?'

'Haven't you heard? Ryan's grandad reported it as cyber-bullying.' I let this piece of false information hang in the air before fleshing out the lie. 'They've already been round my house and confiscated my computer. They probably know by now it wasn't me. Thing is, they've been asking if I can think of anyone else who might have done it.'

For a big lad, Gareth moved incredibly fast. He had me in a headlock, squeezing my neck under his sweaty armpit, before I realized what was happening. He spun me round a couple of times, forcing me to run in order to keep my head attached to my body. I began to think it might have been a mistake to speak to him so soon after eating lunch.

'You say anything to the coppers about me and you'll be sucking your dinner through a straw—up your arse!' said Gareth. I guessed biology wasn't his best subject.

'I just . . . want . . . my phone,' I croaked.

That set off another go on the Gareth roundabout. I was just thinking how much fun all this was, when I heard a familiar voice.

'Malone's coming.'

The grip on my neck released immediately and when I stood up, Psycho was standing next to Gareth watching me. A moment later, Mr Malone appeared.

'Now here's a gathering that makes me very nervous,' he said, his eyes flicking to each of us in turn.

'Actually, I'm just on my way to the library,' I said, seeing an opportunity to retreat while all the parts of my body were still connected.

Gareth glared, but he had no choice but to let me go while Malone was watching. The moment the teacher walked away, I saw Psycho turn to Gareth and say something, then they both glanced in my direction. I should have guessed those two were mates.

In the end I didn't go to the library because I knew Ryan would be in there. It wasn't so much him, as the dirty looks I'd get from everyone else that kept me away.

I caught the whiff of smoke coming up the track and assumed Dad must be burning rubbish. But it was Meg I found standing over the half barrel barbecue in the yard. I was surprised; my sister wasn't exactly the outdoor, making fires type of person.

Meg looked worried for a moment when she heard the gate, then saw it was me.

The smell coming off the barbecue wasn't exactly appetizing, and when I looked inside I saw it was full of clothes. There were no actual flames, but the stripy T-shirt Kris had been wearing when he arrived was going brown and smouldering at the edges.

'What you doing?'

'Burning rubbish,' said Meg, through tight lips.

'That's not very ecological. I thought you were all about saving the planet.'

'Shut up, Oz! I'm really not in the mood.' She dumped a pair of skinny black Levi's onto the fire.

'So . . . have you heard from Kris?'

'He phoned just after you left for school.'

'What did he say?'

Meg put on a pathetic voice. 'He said he was sorry he ran away without me, but he got scared.' She snorted. 'It's like he thinks he's the only one! We were both *scared*, that's why we needed to be together. We could have been all right together, but he had to go and wimp out on me! He said he wasn't ready to be someone's dad! Like being a mum was top of my list of things to do before I'm eighteen!' Meg poked at the clothes with a stick, and by the vicious way she jabbed, I got the feeling she wished Kris was still inside them.

'What are you going to do?'

'Find some petrol.'

'What?'

'For the fire,' said Meg. 'It's not burning properly. Mum should have something in the studio to get it going.'

'I meant, what are you going to do about the baby?'

But she was already walking towards the barn.

I glanced back into the barrel and noticed something shiny poking out from under the jeans. I nudged the fabric to one side and extracted a CD. *LATE NIGHT MIX* was written across it in black marker. I guessed it was a compilation Kris had made for Meg . . . which meant there could be some good stuff on there! I glanced over towards the studio, then pulled the Levi's out of the barbecue. There were more CDs underneath—all labelled by Kris. A couple had already started to melt, the plastic blistering and turning an ugly nicotine brown, but most of them looked all right. It felt like unearthing buried treasure. It was typical of my sister to let emotions get in the way of good music. I was just checking there weren't any more discs at the bottom of the pile, when I found something else.

Apart from one badly singed corner, *Baby's Journey* appeared to have survived. But why was Meg trying to burn it in the first place? Maybe in her blind rage she'd chucked it on there by accident?

I tucked the book under my arm and turned my attention back to the CDs. Apart from *LATE NIGHT MIX*, there was something called *FACTOR 5*, which had a little drawing of a sun with a smiley face; three were simply labelled *FRIS*CO and then a date, which must have come from Kris's club; and finally one called *MEG'S MIX*. This had been at the bottom of the pile and had black scorch marks across it, but other than that, seemed intact. Now all I had to do was get them upstairs without Meg realizing I'd taken them.

I was so engrossed in what I was doing, that the first thing I knew of the van approaching was when the headlights swung across the barns like a searchlight, capturing me in the beam. I opened the gate, then stood back while Dad drove into the yard.

'What's going on?' said Mum, as she got out sniffing the air. 'Is that a fire?'

'Not me!' I said, quickly. 'Meg's getting rid of . . . some stuff!'

Mum walked over to the barbecue and peered at the pile of smouldering clothes. She lifted the edge of the striped T-shirt. 'Doesn't this belong to Kris?'

I shrugged.

Mum's eyes darted towards the CDs in my hand. 'What's that?'

'Just some music.'

'No,' said Mum, pulling the baby book out from under my arm. 'This?' Her eyes widened as she read the cover.

'Found some!' We both turned at the sound of Meg's voice. She was coming out of the studio with a bottle in her hand. She stopped when she saw Mum.

'It's mine,' I said. 'From school. Biology.'

Mum looked at me, then back at the book, then at my sister. 'No!' she said, barely above a whisper. 'Tell me she isn't . . . '

Meg saw what Mum was holding then and bolted towards the house, but not before giving me a look that would have ignited the barbecue in seconds.

'Megan!' Mum went after her.

By the time Dad emerged from the back of the van, they had both disappeared inside.

'Did I miss something?' he said.

'Um . . . you could say that, yeah.'

Before he could ask me any more, Mum appeared at the back door. 'Nigel, I think you'd better come inside.'

I had a feeling that the bomb I'd known would go off had just ticked down to zero.

EIGHTEEN

'SO MANY CHOICES'

First of all there was shouting—mainly Meg and Mum. This was followed by crying—Meg; then talking—Mum and Dad; lots of tea—Dad; and coffee—Mum; and biscuits—also Dad. I was banished to the attic and only able to glean the above information through numerous scouting expeditions to the kitchen on a variety of pretexts. The rest of the time I spent trying out the CDs I'd rescued from Meg's barbecue.

MEG'S MIX turned out to have a crack in it, so that went in the bin. The second *FRISCO* disc made a weird grating sound, but the other four worked perfectly. They weren't quite the goldmine I'd imagined, but then Kris had compiled them with my sister in mind. Not that it mattered. The two surviving *FRISCO* compilations made everything worthwhile. Three Dead Frank tracks and my favourite song by Cigarette UFO, plus a load more great stuff that I'd never heard before. There was still a huge musical hole where my phone should have been, but it was some consolation.

This time I made sure I copied the files to the computer before anything bad happened to the discs. I'd just finished the last one when Dad appeared at the top of the steps.

'Stick your boots on, mate, I need a co-pilot.'

'Where are we going?'

'Very important mission.' He grinned and waved an Indian takeaway menu in the air. 'You can decide what you want on the way.'

Mum and Meg were sitting side by side on the sofa when we walked through the kitchen. Mum had her good arm around my sister who was nestled into her shoulder and looked about twelve years old. I couldn't remember the last time I'd seen them sitting so close to each other, let alone cuddling. The strangest things bring people together. Gonzo Power in action, eh, G!

'So, what d'you fancy?' said Dad, as we drove through the empty village. 'I'm thinking Chicken Jalfrezi—though I do like a good Tandoori mixed grill.' I could see him frowning in the light from the dashboard. 'So many choices.' He sighed.

'I dunno.' Trying to read the menu in the dark, while Dad threw the van around the lanes like a rally driver, was making me feel sick. 'What's that coconut one called?'

'Korma,' said Dad. 'Chicken?'

'Yeah—and some bhajis.'

'Good call! Might have to get an extra bag for the journey home—what d'you say? Got to make sure the hunting party keeps its strength up!'

I knew this whole trip was just an excuse. Dad didn't need me to go with him to pick up a curry. Which meant, he either needed to give Meg and Mum some time alone, or he wanted to talk to me about something. Three guesses what that might be . . .

The problem with Dad is that he's not very good at getting to the point.

'So . . . are you looking forward to being a grandad then?'

The van wavered slightly and Dad coughed. 'Ah . . . so, you worked it out then?' Which is when I remembered I wasn't supposed to know.

'It wasn't hard,' I said, quickly.

'Turns out that's why Kris was up here,' said Dad. 'I suppose we should have guessed there was more to it. But I'll be honest, Oz, I just never imagined Megan would go and get herself pregnant.' He shook his head.

'What did Mum say?'

'What d'you think?'

'Not too keen on the idea?'

He grunted. 'You could say that. The thing is, your mum was very young when we had your sister. Not as young as Megan, but . . . well . . . she doesn't want Meg having to struggle like she did.'

This was news to me. 'Really? How old was she then?'

'Twenty-two. Meg was born three weeks before your mum's final degree show at college. Not surprisingly, she couldn't get everything ready in time.'

I tried to imagine Mum aged twenty-two. I'd seen photos—Dad with hair, Mum looking so young and scarily like my sister—but it was hard matching the faces staring out from those pictures with the people I knew now.

'Your mum gave it her best shot of course. It would take more than a newborn baby to stop her. But she didn't get the grade that everyone had been predicting,' said Dad. 'She's been trying to catch up ever since. That's why this thing at the Sculpture Park means so much to her.'

I winced. Why did everything keep coming back to that?

Balti Towers was on the main road in the centre of Thackett. Dad pulled the van onto the kerb and we stepped out into a steady drizzle. The entrance to the restaurant was flanked by a pair of bejewelled stone elephants and it was warm inside, the dim lighting making the deep red walls appear to glow. We'd barely crossed the threshold before Dad's hand was inside the dish of complimentary Bombay Mix on the counter. I sat down on one of the low squashy chairs by the door, while Dad placed our order.

'They reckon twenty minutes, so I got us a drink,' he said, handing me a bottle with a straw bobbing in the neck.

'Thanks, Grandad!'

Dad raised his eyebrows, then coughed and took a swig of his lager. 'Actually, Oz . . . that's what I wanted to talk to you about.'

'You don't want to be called Grandad? I know, it probably makes you feel really old, yeah?' I placed a hand on his shoulder, my face deadly serious. 'I've got some bad news for you, Dad. You are!'

He half laughed, sighed and gulped some more of his drink. Then he stood up and walked over to the counter for another handful of Bombay Mix.

There was something wrong. I knew the signs.

'Dad, I know you didn't bring me along for the company, so what is it you wanted to talk to me about?'

He looked at me and shook his head. 'That's scary,' he said. 'Your mother does that too. It's like she can read my mind.'

'Well, actually, I can't read yours, so you're going to have to tell me—whatever it is.'

He nodded, swilling the beer around in his glass. 'Your sister's decided to have a termination.'

The door opened and three men walked in, bringing a blast of damp cold air in their wake.

'A termination?'

'It means they stop the pregnancy. An abortion.' Dad blinked and put his glass down on the table. 'Meg had already decided that was what she wanted to do, and your mum and I think it's probably a wise decision.' He sighed, then looked at me and shrugged. 'It's a shame, but . . . like I said, probably the best for everyone . . . in the circumstances.'

'Right.'

'They're both so young,' said Dad. 'Still kids themselves really.'

'Yeah.'

It had never occurred to me that Meg would stop the pregnancy. But then, Dad was right, she was still only seventeen. She wanted to go to university and learn how to save the world. And Kris—I just couldn't picture him stuck in some dingy flat with my sister and a baby. Wasn't that exactly what I'd been trying to tell him the other night?

Had I really influenced Kris's decision to run away? I mean, he must have already had some serious doubts. Meg had just talked him into doing what *she* wanted. So what if I had helped him see the other side? What was wrong with that?

Except now, Meg was going to have a termination. The tiny Foam Shrimp Alien would never grow into Gonzo.

Maybe it didn't matter. It was probably best for everyone. Wasn't that what Dad had said?

NINETEEN

A BOY WITH BLUE HAIR

There was already a long line of people waiting outside the club where Kris was DJ. It felt good getting waved past the queue to be let in ahead of everyone else.

The bouncer pointed down a corridor. 'Straight down there, mate!'

I could hear the distant thump of music somewhere deep in the building—Cyclops Dog doing their soundcheck. Kris had invited me down early so I could meet Michael Death, Dead Frank's legendary bass player. I couldn't decide if I wanted to throw up because I was nervous or excited.

The walls of the corridor were black, as was the ceiling and the floor, though every square centimetre had graffiti scratched into the surface. After a few metres the passage-way turned a sharp left and went down a flight of steps. I guessed this was the backstage area that only artists and special invited guests, like yours truly, got to see.

Finally I came to a set of double doors and pushed through into a large dimly lit hall. There was a stage at one end, but the place was deserted—no sign of Kris or Cyclops Dog. I could still hear music, but it sounded further away now. I was about to go back, to make sure I hadn't taken a wrong turn, when I noticed somebody sitting on the edge of the stage. Thinking they might be able to give me directions, I walked over and saw it was just a kid. He looked about seven years old and had bright blue hair, which struck me as odd.

As I got closer, he waved and jumped down. 'Hello, Uncle Oz.'

I stared at him. 'What did you say?'

'I said, *hello, Uncle* Oz.' And he waved again.

I moved closer. 'Gonzo?'

A huge grin spread across his face and he nodded.

'I don't understand.'

'You're dreaming, stupid,' he said. 'I mean, did you really think you'd get to meet Michael Death in real life?'

'I haven't even met him in my dream yet!' I pointed out. 'Anyway, what are you doing here? Aren't you a bit young to be out by yourself?'

He shrugged. 'You're here.'

'Yeah, but . . . ' And then it started to snow, except the snow was black.

I held out my hand, catching a few of the flakes as they fluttered down. It was ash, from a bonfire. I frowned, then caught the dry scent of smoke in the air.

'Quick!' I said. 'We've got to get out of here. I think the building's on fire!' But the boy with blue hair had vanished. 'Gonzo!' I shouted—

I woke up with my face pressed against the pages of *Baby's Journey,* open on my pillow. Cyclops Dog were still playing in my headphones. I pulled out the buds and sat up.

I'd found the book in the bin. Dad had made me take all the curry cartons and the little plastic bags of salad out to the yard. When I opened the lid, the charred remains of Meg's barbecue was crammed in there, with *Baby's Journey* sitting on top of the pile.

Even at the time, I wasn't sure why I stuffed the book inside my jumper and sneaked it up to my room. I'd sat in bed looking again at the flick-book Foam Shrimp Alien, trying to work out which drawing looked most like you.

The book was open at a page showing a picture of a baby curled up next to a giant banana. *Baby is now approximately half the size of a banana*, said the text underneath. *He will grow about five centimetres in the next four weeks and become much more active, even trying out a few different facial expressions.*

I swore and closed the book with a snap, sending more ash fluttering onto my pillow. If I hadn't been too lazy to move, I would have put *Baby's Journey* back in the bin. Instead, I slid it under the bed, plugged my earphones in and clicked *play* on the laptop. I lay down and shut my eyes, but the smell of damp ash lingered in the air, while the blue-haired boy grinned at me from the darkness.

TWENTY

'JUST SAY *THANK YOU* AND DON'T ASK QUESTIONS'

I was half expecting another close encounter with the sofa cushions as a reward for spilling Meg's secret, but if anything my sister seemed relieved. The termination appointment wasn't for another week, but already it felt like Meg was no longer pregnant. Nobody mentioned it, and life carried on as though nothing had ever happened. The weird thing was—*I* couldn't stop thinking about it.

Even though I no longer had to wrestle the Cramp Bed each night, I hadn't been sleeping too well. The boy with the blue hair was making regular appearances in my dreams, throwing himself wilfully into harm's way, just to taunt me. I'd wake up, not sure if I'd been shouting *Gonzo!* out loud, or just in the dream. Once awake, I found it hard to get back to sleep again. I'd spent the last two nights sitting up in bed listening to music on my laptop. Which probably explained why it felt as though somebody had crept into my room during the early hours and glued weights to my eyelids.

It had to stop.

What was my problem? Meg was having a termination so there wouldn't be a real baby, yet I couldn't even get rid of the imaginary one in my head.

Now, don't take that the wrong way, G—but you need to see it from my point of view. I seriously thought I was going mad. I had all the signs: voices in my head, weird dreams, talking to myself, not sleeping. The situation was getting desperate and it wasn't as if there was anybody I could talk to about it.

I still hadn't heard anything back from Jack, even though I'd emailed him three times from Mum's computer. There had been no replacement Dead Frank in the post either.

The day after my failed attempt to scare Gareth into returning my mobile, I found a drinking straw sellotaped to my locker. I guessed it was some kind of low-budget, mafia style warning, and actually quite clever for Gareth. While it didn't have the same shock value as waking up with a horse's head, the message was no less clear.

Just in case I'd missed the subtlety of the straw though, Gareth maintained a steady stream of low-level menacing for the rest of the week: head shaking, meaningful looks and gestures, even a couple of dead-legs in the corridor when I hadn't seen him coming.

All things considered it had been quite a week. I was glad when Saturday finally arrived.

I was on my own in the kitchen, leisurely mopping up the remains of a bacon sandwich, when somebody knocked on the window. I looked up and saw Psycho Skinner peering through the glass at me. As I was the only person in the room and she'd already seen me, I had no choice but to open the door.

'Nice jim-jams,' she said, looking me up and down.

I'd forgotten I was still in my pyjamas—an ancient pair with cartoon skeletons all over them. I quickly checked to make sure my fly wasn't hanging open. 'Um . . . these are really old—my others are in the wash.'

Psycho nodded. 'Right. Save your silk ones for entertaining, do you?'

My cheeks cranked up a notch from pink to crimson. 'Mum's not here,' I said, not bothering to hide the irritation in my voice.

'That's OK. It's you I want.'

'Me?'

Psycho reached into her pocket and for a second I almost expected to find a gun pointed at me. What I saw instead was perhaps an even bigger shock.

'This is the phone you've been hassling me about, right?' said Psycho, holding out my mobile.

'Where d'you get it? From Gareth?'

Psycho sighed and leant towards me. 'Word of advice, Marcus. Just say *thank you* and don't ask questions.'

'Right . . . um . . . thanks.'

'You're welcome.' She turned and whistled to The Beast, and then they both strolled out of the yard.

There had to be a catch. It was some kind of trick—Gareth and Psycho teaming up for a final slamdown. But when I switched the phone on everything seemed to be working, and there were no obvious signs of tampering. All the music was still there, my playlists, the video of Frog and the wheelie-bin . . . which was when it occurred to me that my old friends had probably been trying to get in touch.

Sure enough, when I checked, I had twelve unanswered texts. Five were from Dad, who had taken a while to remember I'd lost my phone. One was from the phone company telling me my credit was low, another from some random website trying to sell me something. The other four were from Ryan—sent before he'd found out about the photos, of course. Nothing from Jack, Tuna, or Frog—but then I'd told Jack about my phone, so he'd known there was no point in texting me.

I sent Jack a message to let him know I was back online, then spent the rest of the afternoon copying the music files from my phone to my laptop, while Dead Frank rattled the tiny plastic speakers. I was so happy, I didn't give another thought to how, and perhaps more importantly, why, Psycho had got my phone back. It might have made things a lot easier if I had.

On Monday morning Gareth came into school with a split and swollen lip. He claimed to have done it during rugby training, but by lunchtime there were whispers going round that he'd been involved in an encounter with Psycho. I'd already noticed that Gareth was giving me an unusually wide berth, making do with sneering glances, rather than the up-close-and-personal treatment I was used to.

This time I did stop to wonder what exactly had gone on between them. As far as I understood, my relationship with

Psycho was based on a mutual dislike that suited us both. So why had she gone out of her way to help me? Perhaps she thought it was the only way to stop me hassling her. Or maybe she just didn't like Gareth. In the end I decided it didn't matter. I had my phone back and, for the time being at least, Gareth was keeping his distance. I decided to take Psycho's advice—just say thank you and not ask questions.

I'd just got off the bus, when I saw Meg walking through the village ahead of me.

'What you doing here?' I said, when I caught up.

'I live here, Oz. Remember?'

'No, I mean . . . like, now.'

Meg let out an exasperated breath. 'I've just been to see Don at the pub. I had to tell him I can't work tomorrow night.'

'Why not?'

'What's it got to do with you?'

'Just making conversation.'

She sighed. 'Dad's taking me to the clinic tomorrow. For the termination.'

'Oh . . . right.'

'I'm scared, Oz.'

I looked at her. Being scared wasn't something Meg would normally admit to, especially not to me. 'Why? Will it hurt?'

'I don't know. I don't care about that.'

'So what are you scared of?'

Meg stopped walking and turned to face me. 'What if I'm doing the wrong thing, Oz? What if I regret it afterwards?'

'I thought you wanted to get rid of him.'

'It's not that I want to *get rid of him* . . . it. I just . . . ' She gnawed the edge of her thumbnail. 'I can't look after a baby on my own, can I? I mean, it wouldn't be fair . . . to the baby.'

I shrugged. 'Mum and Dad would help though, wouldn't they? And me! Though, don't expect me to have anything to do with waste disposal. That's definitely your department.'

She laughed, then stopped abruptly and put her hand to her mouth and I could tell she was trying not to cry.

'You're only seventeen,' I said. 'How can you be someone's mum? I mean, you can hardly look after yourself!'

This time when she laughed, a big fat tear spilt from her eye and rolled down her cheek.

'Idiot,' she said, sniffing and wiping her eyes with a tissue. 'Imagine if I had a baby and it turned out like you!'

'Nah,' I said. 'I've seen Gonzo—he's OK. Mental hair though—bright blue it is. And he's out all hours, getting into all sorts of trouble. I blame the parents.'

Meg looked at me. 'What *are* you on about?'

'Been having some seriously weird dreams,' I said, as we started walking again. 'I mean, I know in real life Gonzo's like the size of my thumb or something, but in my dreams he's this little kid, about seven years old. It's doing my head in.'

'I sometimes wonder if we're related,' said Meg. 'Or maybe Mum inhaled too much paint thinners when she was pregnant with you.'

'Nah, it's just a reaction to a lifetime spent with you. It's enough to send anyone round the bend.'

Meg aimed a kick at me and missed by a mile. But she was still laughing and didn't look quite so scared any more.

I started telling her about Psycho turning up with my phone and all the stuff with Gareth, and then out of nowhere, just as we reached the gate, she said:

'Blue hair?'

I stopped. 'What?'

'You said, in your dreams, Gonzo had blue hair.' It was the first time she'd ever used that name herself.

'Yeah. Like a mop, sticking out all over the place it was.'

She smiled. 'I always wanted blue hair, but Mum wouldn't let me.' Then she shrugged and walked towards the house.

TWENTY-ONE

THE MOMENT I REALIZED WHAT AN IDIOT I'D BEEN

Meg and Dad had already left by the time I got up for school. Mum didn't say much while we ate breakfast, but then neither did I. What was there to say? It occurred to me that the next time I sat at the kitchen table everything would be back to normal. It seemed strange to think that something that would have changed all of our lives for ever, could just disappear.

I had English last period before lunch. We'd been reading this book where the main character commits a horrible crime and then feels guilty. The whole story is in the form of a letter, written by the perpetrator to the victim, trying to explain why he did it.

'I want you to write a letter,' said Miss Davies. 'To someone you have wronged. Think about who you are writing to and what you have done to them. Why are you writing? Is it to ask for forgiveness? To help them understand? Or just so you feel better?'

Gareth put his hand up. 'Can't we just text, miss? Nobody actually writes letters these days.'

'No, Gareth, you can't just text. You don't have this person's number.'

'What if you can't think of anyone?' asked one of the girls.

Miss Davies raised an eyebrow. 'Then you have to make something up! Use your imagination.'

A collective groan rumbled across the room.

I picked up my pen and stared at the blank sheet of paper. It was obvious who I should be writing to. I looked across the classroom to the curly head bent low over his desk. But a letter of apology to Ryan would be nothing short of suicide. There was a chance Miss Davies would ask us to read out what we had written. It didn't bear thinking about.

The room had gone quiet, apart from the scratching of pens and the occasional exchange of whispers.

Use your imagination. Make something up.

How could I? When my mind kept drifting back to Meg and Dad.

Then, almost without thinking, I started—

Message to Gonzo, I wrote. *Dear* sounded too old-fashioned.

Listen, G—this is important and there isn't much time.

I knew I was probably too late already. But then, it wasn't as if you were ever going to read this. It was like those times I'd talked to you in my head, as though I could transmit the words to you somehow, just by thinking.

I want you to know what really happened, because things weren't supposed to end like this, I wrote. *I blame Marcel*

Duchamp, but he's dead, so there's not much anybody can do to him now. When he drew a moustache and a goatee beard on a copy of the Mona Lisa—which is probably the most famous painting in the world—he said he did it because he wanted to challenge people's perception of what art could be.

He was lying.

He did it because it was funny. Moustaches are funny. End of story.

Except in this case, G—it was just the beginning.

But what *was* the end? Had Gonzo's story already finished?

That was the moment, G. The moment I realized what an idiot I'd been. Now I knew why the boy with the blue hair had been stomping around in my dreams; why your voice kept arriving uninvited into my head; why I couldn't stop reading that stupid book. I couldn't let your story end like that. I had to do something.

If I wasn't already too late.

I don't know what happened when I got up and ran out of the classroom. I think Miss Davies called after me, but I didn't hear what she said. I remember being outside, tearing through the gates, running like I'd run from The Beast, like my life depended on it—or yours.

At the corner of the road I pulled out my phone and dialled Dad's mobile. When he answered, I was almost too scared to speak.

'Dad!'

'Oz?'

'Where are you?'

'Just having a bite to eat before we head home. What's wrong, mate?'

Before we head home. I was too late.

'Oz?'

My throat had closed up. It felt dry and hot. I wouldn't have been able to speak, even if there'd been words to say. But there weren't. I was too late. It was over.

'Oz? You still there, mate? What's going on?'

'I'm too late!' I said.

'Too late? For what? Did you miss the bus?'

I didn't answer.

'Are you at school?' said Dad. 'What's going on? Talk to me, mate!'

'I didn't think you'd be coming home yet,' I said. 'I thought I still had time.'

'Well . . . ' Dad lowered his voice. 'Your sister had a change of heart. She decided she couldn't go through with it, so . . . we're on our way back.'

It took a moment for Dad's words to sink in. 'You mean, she's still pregnant?'

I heard him chuckle at the other end of the line. 'It looks like I'm going to be a grandad after all!'

Mr Malone was waiting for me when I walked back through the school gates. I followed him to his office and saw my bag on the floor by the window. It made me wonder who had packed up my stuff. I couldn't imagine there would have been too many volunteers.

I didn't bother trying to make up a reason why I'd suddenly bolted out of English. I told him the truth. He seemed surprised, then asked me to promise that if I ever felt the urge to run out of school again, I would go and talk to him first. I nodded, but I wasn't really listening.

You were safe, G, and that was all that mattered.

THE MIDDLE

G MINUS 199

TWENTY-TWO

SOME WEIRD SIGN OF AFFECTION

Finding out you were still on your way changed everything, G. I felt like I'd been given a second chance—an opportunity to put things right. I was starting to realize that nothing happens in isolation. There's always a chain of events leading up to it. The trouble was, there had been too many times recently, when, if you looked down the chain, you'd find me there at the start. But all that was going to change.

So when I stepped out into the icy drizzle sweeping across the quad three days later, I was filled with an unfamiliar sense of hope and well-being.

The punch came out of nowhere. I saw a blur of movement, then something hard connected with my face. I staggered backwards, tasting blood, and put a hand to my mouth. Then I saw Ryan, standing in front of me with his fists clenched. His eyes were wild, but at the same time he looked like he was about to cry.

'What d'you do that for?' I said, looking at the smear of blood on my fingers.

'You deserved it,' said Ryan. 'For what you did.'

I shrugged. 'OK. You're probably right.'

He looked surprised, and then seemed to notice the crowd forming rapidly around us, jostling and shouting.

'Hit him again, Frodo!' Hands reached out, pushing Ryan towards me, and when I tried to back away, the bodies behind blocked me in.

'Go on, Kecks! Don't be scared.'

Ryan looked suddenly terrified, his eyes darting from me to the crowd and back again. I guessed all he'd wanted was one punch—payback, then walk away—not this: a full-blown public fight. Surely one of the teachers would hear the noise and come along to break it up soon. I was no more of a fighter than Ryan. The whole thing was ridiculous.

Then someone shoved him and he slipped on the wet tarmac. Ryan's arm shot out as he lost balance and his elbow caught me in the eye. I didn't mean to hit him back—it was instinct. I didn't even know I was going to do it, until I felt my fist connect with something hard. There was an audible crunch and the hard thing suddenly became soft and mushy. Ryan yelped and reeled backwards, clutching his face with both hands. Blood started dripping through his fingers and the crowd gasped.

'He's crying—look!'

'That's a busted nose!'

'Where's Gandalf when you need him, eh!'

'Miss Davies is coming!'

The circle dissolved as fast as it had formed.

'Ryan! I'm sorry! It was an accident!' I tried to walk over to him, but the teacher stepped between us.

'Stay right where you are, Marcus!' She turned to Ryan. 'Let me have a look.' I watched Ryan lower his hands and my stomach lurched when I saw the mess I'd made of his face. 'Right, we need to get you to the nurse. I think that could be broken.'

'It was an accident!' I said again.

Miss Davies gave me a disgusted look, then marched us past the lines of gawping faces. Gareth could barely stand he was laughing so hard. When we got inside, Miss Davies told me to wait by Mr Malone's office while she took Ryan to the medical room. I watched them go, trying to work out what the hell had just happened.

'I thought you and Ryan were mates?' Dad glanced up from the letter Mr Malone had sent home, explaining the reasons I'd been put on report. 'It says here you could have been expelled for fighting.'

'I know, but it wasn't a fight. It was an accident.'

'How can you punch someone in the face by accident?'

I tried to explain about the slippery ground and the pushing.

'But I don't understand how it started in the first place, Oz.'

Of course the answer to that lay at the end of another chain of blame, not one I wanted Dad to rattle.

'We had an argument,' I said. 'It doesn't matter.'

He frowned. 'This is serious, Oz. Getting put on report is your last chance. You mess up again and they'll chuck you out.'

'I'm sorry,' I said. 'I know it's my last chance. I'm trying . . . to put things right.'

'Glad to hear it.' Dad sighed and put the letter back into the envelope. 'Your mum's not going to be happy. She could do without this right now.'

'Maybe you don't have to tell her?'

He raised an eyebrow. 'I'm sorry, mate, you're just going to have to take whatever's coming to you on this one. Just do me a favour and try to stay out of trouble for a bit though, eh? What with Meg's baby, your mum's crash and everything, I'm not sure how much more I can take. I haven't got any hair left to fall out!'

To say Mum wasn't going to be happy was like describing the North Pole as *a bit chilly*. Mum was going to go into orbit on this one. Ever since Meg had come back from the termination with a baby still on board, the atmosphere at home had definitely gone down a degree or two, and it had nothing to do with the fact it was winter and we had no heating.

For once though, G—I was lucky. My letter from school arrived on the same day as a piece of good news for Mum.

'I'm in the local paper!' she said, spreading the pages out on the kitchen table.

LOCAL SCULPTOR CREATES A BUZZ read the headline. Underneath was a colour photo of Mum in the studio with the giant wasp. Somehow they'd managed to make it look as though the insect was actually hovering in the air—but that wasn't what caught my attention. Standing next to Mum, on the other side of the yellow and black striped abdomen, was Psycho. The caption read: *Sculptor Dawn Osbourne in her Slowleigh studio with assistant Isobel Skinner.*

'Good picture,' said Dad.

Mum nodded. 'I know it's only a local paper, but Geraint said he's been talking to a journalist from *The Sunday Times*. He's hoping we might get a mention the weekend before the opening.'

'Great,' said Dad, and then Mum's mobile rang.

'Geraint! Yes, I've just seen it!' She turned and headed for the back door.

'I see Mum's Little Helper managed to muscle her way into the picture,' muttered Meg. 'Who does she think she looks like? Lara Croft!'

I picked up the paper and looked more closely at the photo. Psycho's overalls were undone and rolled down to the waist, revealing a grubby grey vest that showed off her muscles . . . and stuff. I'd never thought about it before, but now Meg mentioned it, she did look a bit like Lara Croft.

As there wasn't much point in grounding me—I never went out, except to go to school—Dad had sentenced me to a week's Slave Duty, which basically meant that all the rubbish jobs around the house had my name on them. This included taking food and drink out to the studio.

With the Sculpture Park exhibition only a few weeks away, Mum was virtually living in there. She was too stressed to stop and come into the house to eat with the rest of us, so Dad kept up a regular supply of sandwiches, drinks, and biscuits, which I had to deliver.

That night he'd made a mountain of sandwiches from the chicken left over from dinner. He placed the plate on a tray alongside two mugs of steaming black coffee and handed it to me. 'Take these out to your mum and Isobel for us, mate.'

As always, the moment I stepped outside, The Beast was there, sniffing at the tray and drooling all over my trainers. I was tempted to aim a swift kick at the two doggie nuggets dangling between his legs, then remembered I was supposed to be finding ways to say *thank you* to Psycho, not kicking her dog in the nuts. Which is when I had the genius idea.

Having delivered the sandwiches, I went back inside and retrieved the chicken carcass Dad had just dumped in the bin, then opened the back door again.

'Hey, dog!' I said. 'Lucky!'

The Beast shot out of the barn and hurtled towards me. I dumped the chicken remains onto the ground and stepped out of the way. Seconds later, there was a loud crunch as the dog's jaws closed around the bones, followed by a yell. I looked up and saw Psycho sprinting from the studio, shouting at the dog. She grabbed his collar and pulled him away.

'What do you think you're doing?' she screamed.

'Just giving your dog something to eat,' I said. 'I thought he'd like it.' The Beast looked as confused as I was.

'Are you a complete idiot?'

The back door opened then and Dad stuck his head out to see what all the shouting was about. 'Ah,' he said. 'You're not supposed to give chicken bones to dogs, mate. They can choke.'

'How was I supposed to know that? I was just trying to be nice.'

Psycho was fussing over The Beast, but he looked fine to me.

'He doesn't seem to be showing any adverse affects,' said Dad, giving Lucky's ears a scratch.

'No thanks to Brainless!' said Psycho.

'I was only trying to be nice to that stupid mutt,' I said, once Dad and I were back inside.

'No harm done,' he said. 'You'll know next time.'

I snorted. 'Did you hear what she called me?'

Dad grinned. 'I reckon she fancies you, mate.'

'What?'

'It's a classic sign. Have you never seen one of those films when two people spend the first hour and a half hating each other, then right at the end realize they're actually madly in love. Happens all the time.'

For once I was lost for words.

'Why else d'you think she comes round here so much? You don't really believe it's just to help your mother out do you?'

'Well . . . yeah.' But hadn't I thought the same thing? That Psycho must have some dark ulterior motive for coming round. I'd just never imagined it might be me!

Then I remembered the day she'd run at me with the hammer, how she had pushed me back against the wall, her body pressed into mine. Had that really been some weird sign of affection? And then there was the whole business with Gareth and the phone. Hadn't I been struggling to find a reason why Psycho would go out of her way to get my phone back and give Gareth a fat lip? Fancying me would be a reason . . .

But that thought was way more terrifying than the idea she wanted to kill me.

TWENTY-THREE

A PEACE OFFERING

It had been raining non-stop for about a week. I'd forgotten what it felt like not to be damp and cold all the time. Dad was supposed to be getting the central heating finished so the house would be warm for Christmas, but when I got back from school I found him in the nursery again.

To be honest, G, it looked a right mess. A spider of wires hung down from the ceiling, with more snaking along the walls in wide grooves cut into the plaster. Half the floorboards were up, and there were bits of pipe and tools lying everywhere. It was the same all over the house. You only had to put something down for a few minutes and it would be covered in a film of dust—even the air tasted gritty.

Dad was standing in the middle of it all, a mug of tea in his hand, staring out of the window deep in thought. He looked round when I walked in.

'What do you think sounds better? Gramp, Grandad, or Pop?' Since discovering he was going to be a grandad after all, Dad had gone baby mad. It was all he ever talked about.

I shrugged. 'I can't quite see you as Pop, somehow . . .'

He laughed. 'Hey, I found some great wallpaper! I think you'll approve.' He lifted a dustsheet from an amorphous pile in the corner of the room and pulled out a multi-coloured tube. 'Muppets!' He grinned. 'You think Meg'll like it?'

'Probably not. But if it's already on the wall, what's she going to do?' I turned the roll until I found a picture of Gonzo wearing a top hat, but it didn't really look like you, G.

'Do you think you'll get it ready in time?' I asked, handing back the wallpaper.

'Yeah! No problem. Should have the re-wiring done by the end of next week. Get the rest of the pipes down . . . ' He grinned. 'How about you? Anything happen today that I don't want to know about?'

I shook my head.

'You made up with Ryan yet?'

'He won't have anything to do with me.' I sat down on a roll of carpet. 'Can't say I blame him though.'

Thanks to me, Ryan was now known throughout Crawdale High as Frodopo. The name, coined by Gareth no doubt, was an amalgamation of Frodo the hobbit and Po, from *Kung-Fu Panda*. Apparently when Ryan slipped during our fight and elbowed me in the face, it had looked like he was attempting Kung-Fu. When he returned to school the next day with two black eyes looking like a panda, the legend of Frodopo—the Kung-Fu Hobbit—was born. I actually thought that *Frodopo* was a better nickname than *Kecks*, but Ryan didn't quite see it that way. At least I don't think he did. It was hard to tell, as Ryan had only spoken to me once since the fight, and that had been to tell me to get lost—or words to that effect.

'Well, you know what they say—' Dad put down his mug. 'Actions speak louder than words.'

I groaned. 'Yeah, but what does that actually *mean*?'

'It means—in the context of your current predicament—that maybe Ryan isn't interested in you *saying* how sorry you are, that maybe you need to *do* something to prove it.'

'Like what?'

'I don't know, he's your mate. What does he like?'

'Books . . . films—but he's got gazillions of those already.'

'Well,' said Dad. 'Is there anything he needs?'

'Needs?' How was I supposed to know? Everyone kept going on about how me and Ryan were mates, but in truth I hardly knew him.

And then it hit me.

'Music! He needs music!'

'Music?'

'Seriously, Dad. The kid's aurally deprived. All he listens to is the Beatles!'

'What's wrong with the Beatles?'

'That's exactly my point! Thanks, Dad.'

I waited for my laptop to groan into life and began planning the playlists I was going to make for Ryan. They would form the basis of a complete musical re-education—something he was in desperate need of. More importantly, they would be a peace offering to show how sorry I was.

I'd start off fairly mainstream—a few of the retro tracks from the Kris collection. Then I'd lay some of the more obscure stuff on him—Dead Frank, of course, some Cigarette UFO, maybe even a track or two by Cyclops Dog. I'd be introducing him to a whole new world of music.

It took all night, but when I'd finished, the memory stick was full. Over eight hours of music in six carefully structured playlists, all labelled and numbered in the order I thought Ryan should listen to them. I was fairly confident that if he followed my instructions and worked his way through in the prescribed order, he would come out the other side a whole new person.

How could he fail to forgive me after that?

TWENTY-FOUR

A WHOLE NEW PERSPECTIVE ON THINGS

We were late. The special Private View opening for Mum's exhibition at the Sculpture Park was due to start in just over an hour, but Dad couldn't get his trousers to fasten. The problem was, he was trying to squeeze into an ancient suit that looked like it had been stolen from a much smaller man.

'I swear these trousers have shrunk,' he said. 'They fitted perfectly last time I wore them.'

'When was that? Last century?'

Dad frowned and threaded a belt around his waist. 'There you go—sorted! If I leave my jacket done up, nobody will know.'

'Why do we have to dress up, anyway?' I said. The whole *smart clothes* thing had been sprung on me at the last minute.

'Posh do, this, mate! We've got to make an effort.'

'I don't see how wearing my school shirt and trousers is making much of an effort. I wear them every day.'

'It's smart,' he said. 'At least it won't be too bad if I give that shirt an iron. Here, try this tie on.' He handed me a black and white monstrosity that was supposed to look like a piano keyboard.

'I thought you said *smart*—not fancy dress.'

Dad looked hurt. 'It's a design classic that! Dead fashionable. I used to get comments about that tie every time I wore it.'

'You don't say.'

'Well, which one do you want then? You choose.' Dad's collection of ties was displayed on the bed. The least offensive was a plain black one. It was the width of a small table tennis bat, but if I reversed the thing it might not look too bad.

'I save that for funerals,' said Dad.

'Perfect!'

When we finally climbed into the van, I was surprised to see that Dad had cleaned it out for the occasion. Then a couple of minutes into the journey we stopped and I found out why.

It took me a moment before I realized that the person getting into the back with me—the person wearing high-heels and stinking of perfume—was Psycho. I should have guessed she'd be coming with us. I was surprised she hadn't brought The Beast along.

'You two behave yourselves back there,' said Dad, giving me a wink before closing the door.

Psycho sat down on the wheel arch opposite and grunted a greeting. I was glad that the road noise and general rattling made it difficult to talk, not that either of us appeared to have anything to say. Mind you, it didn't stop my heart bouncing around my ribcage like a startled bluebottle. It was the first time we'd been alone together since Dad had planted the idea that Psycho might actually like me, and I could feel my palms beginning to sweat. The perfume she was wearing smelt vaguely of coconut, which made me think of chicken korma, which in turn reminded me how hungry I was. The Great Tie and Trousers Panic had meant we'd run out of time to eat. Dad had promised there would be food at the party though.

To be honest, G, the name *Crawdale Sculpture Park* had conjured up visions of a field the size of a football pitch, similar to the one at the back of the Beckett Arms, with Mum's sculptures scattered across it. But when I got out of the van, I found myself looking up at a large modern building made of glass and metal. The path leading to the entrance was illuminated by a series of stone pillars topped with flickering blue flames. A huge white banner had been hung above the doors, with INSECT NATION and Mum's name in large black letters, next to a picture showing part of the wasp's head. Underneath in smaller type it said: *"It is not the strongest of the species that survives, nor the most intelligent, but the one most adaptable to change."—Charles Darwin.*

'Wow!' said Dad, surreptitiously checking the belt on his trousers. 'Impressive!'

We'd barely stepped through the glass doors when a man in a pale cream suit rushed forward and kissed Mum on both cheeks.

Geraint shook hands with each of us, then offered to take our coats. It was only when I saw Mum in her floor length black dress that I realized she was no longer wearing her arm cast. I was so used to seeing her in overalls and an apron, with her hair tied up in a scarf, it was quite a shock. But Mum's transformation was nothing compared to Psycho's.

Meg snorted and muttered, 'Oops, I think someone forgot her trousers!'

I looked across in time to see Psycho hand Geraint the long coat she had been wearing, revealing a short silver dress that shimmered under the lights. Her hair, freed from its ponytail, hung past her shoulders in dark waves. I swallowed.

Meg was clutching her coat closed and seemed reluctant to hand it over. When she finally swore under her breath and took it off, I could see why. She was wearing an ill-advised orange dress and tights combo, and with your bump now visible, G, she reminded me of an upside-down Space Hopper.

We followed Geraint into a cavernous hall, two sides of which were made entirely of glass. Through the windows I could see a paved terrace bathed in blue light and lawns stretching into darkness beyond. There was a balcony overlooking the gallery and huge sails suspended from a ceiling so high it made you dizzy just to look. And all around, gleaming in the lights, were Mum's metal insects. I had to agree with Dad—it was impressive.

The centre of the space was dominated by a sculpture I hadn't seen before, though I recognized the angular structure that I'd mistaken for a badly erected tent in the studio. I now saw that they were the limbs of a huge creature, crouching like it was about to pounce across the room. It had a skinny ribbed body and in front of the four legs on the ground, two more bent back on themselves—or maybe they were pincers, I wasn't sure. Curved antennae protruded from the top of its head, while the glowing red eyes seemed to follow me as I moved across the floor. It was even more creepy than the wasp.

'What is it?' I asked Meg, but it was Psycho who answered.

'Praying mantis,' she said. 'The female eats the male after mating. It's all part of the theme—how the human race is consuming itself and the planet to extinction.'

'Cheerful stuff,' I said, stepping away from the cloud of coconut perfume.

The problems really started when the photographer arrived. After taking a few shots of Mum next to the wasp, he moved on to some of her and Geraint under the mantis. Then he asked if he could have one of Mum and her daughter, so Meg stepped forward.

The photographer frowned. 'Ah, no . . . sorry, I meant . . . ' And he pointed to Psycho.

Meg looked like she was ready to impale him on his own tripod, but Mum just smiled and said, 'This is Isobel, my assistant—my right hand—well, left hand actually!' She laughed. 'My daughter doesn't really get involved with my work.'

'And you don't really get involved with my life,' muttered Meg, though I don't think anybody else heard her.

Then Mum started going on about how great Psycho was. 'I couldn't have done any of this without Izzy,' she said, while the photographer snapped away. To be fair, Psycho looked slightly uncomfortable with all the attention and stood there awkwardly while Meg growled into her fist behind me.

When he'd finally finished capturing Psycho and her silver dress from every angle, Mum asked if we could have a picture of the family.

The photo is in a frame on the wall in the studio. It's not a classic, though it pretty much captures us as we were on that night. Meg looking like she's about to headbutt someone and Dad holding onto his trousers. In my black tie and white school shirt, I'm doing a good impression of a waiter who stumbled into the picture by accident. It's a nice one of Mum though, and the first family portrait with you in, G!

Three hours later I was bored. There's a finite amount of fun to be had in a room full of giant metal insects and people talking about art. Mum was still surrounded by admirers and Dad had gone off in search of canapés. I helped myself to another glass of fizzy orange from the buffet table and went to look for Meg.

I found her upstairs on the balcony, sitting in a large armchair with her shoes off.

'What you doing up here?'

'Hiding. My feet hurt and I've had enough of people staring at my bump.' She rested a hand on her belly.

I leaned over the balcony and wished I hadn't. 'Whoa! Long way down!'

'How many of those have you had?' said Meg, nodding at the glass I was holding.

'Three . . . four, maybe?' I shrugged. 'Can't remember.'

'Three or four!' said Meg. 'You know that's Bucks Fizz.'

'What?'

'Champagne and orange juice. It's alcohol, Oz. You're drunk.'

I sniffed the liquid and took another gulp. 'That's why it tastes funny. I just thought it was some kind of posh fizzy orange.'

'From specially imported fizzy oranges,' said Meg.

I laughed.

'I don't blame you. I wish I could get drunk.'

I held out the glass. 'Go for your life, sis! Have one on me.'

'I can't. You're not supposed to drink when you're pregnant.'

'Oh, yeah, I forgot.' I looked at the glass, shrugged and downed it in one.

'Bloody hell, Oz!'

I burped and grinned. 'Time for a refill, I think!'

Psycho Skinner was standing alone by the buffet table when I got downstairs. She did look kind of amazing in that silver dress—Lara Croft and then some! It wouldn't hurt to say *hello*—see friendly, not cocky. I mean, she had got my phone back and well . . . what could go wrong this time? It wasn't like there was any danger I could accidentally kill her dog or anything.

So I grabbed two glasses of the fizzy orange and walked over.

'I got you a drink,' I said, holding out the glass a bit too enthusiastically and splashing half of it over my hand. 'Whoops!' I laughed.

Psycho frowned.

'Take it!' I said, then moved closer so I could whisper. 'It tastes a bit funny, but don't worry. It's made from special fizzy oranges. Imported!'

She looked at me for a moment, then took both glasses and put them onto the table without drinking any.

'What you doing?'

'Come on,' she said. 'Let's go outside for some fresh air.' I felt her hand on my arm and was enveloped in a cloud of perfume.

'You know what?' I said, as we stepped onto the terrace. 'You smell really nice tonight. A bit like . . . ' I fumbled for the word and came up with 'chicken korma'. Even as I said it, I had a feeling it wasn't quite right.

'Thanks,' she said. 'Of course, I did it all for you, Marcus.'

So it was true!

I felt like I should say something in response and glanced at her for inspiration. The silver dress glowed like mercury in the moonlight, flowing over her body as she moved.

'I like your dress,' I said.

Psycho looked at me. 'Thanks.'

Emboldened by such a promising start, I kept talking. 'I've got to admit it was a bit of a surprise though. I mean, don't take this the wrong way, but I thought you were like some total psycho nutter, but you're actually OK. I mean, you actually look really good when you make the effort.'

We had left behind the pool of light on the terrace and were walking across one of the endless lawns. Apart from the distant glow of the moon, it was completely dark. I wondered where she was leading me and felt a strange shivery twist in my stomach.

Shapes began emerging from the gloom—a tall sculpture, like a tree made of metal arrows, reared up in front of us. When we reached it, Psycho turned me around to face her. Even in the dark I could see the outline of her features, and was very aware of how close we were standing.

Was she going to kiss me? Did I want her to kiss me?

The question caused chaos in my Bucks Fizzed brain.

I closed my eyes as I felt her hands on my shoulders, sliding down my back towards my waist. I swallowed and my question was answered with an unequivocal . . . YES!

When I felt myself being lifted, I thought at first it was my imagination, then something cold struck my back and I opened my eyes. At the same moment Psycho let go. For a split second I was falling, then the waistband of my trousers tightened and I was clamped in an eye-watering wedgie. It took me a few seconds to realize I was dangling by my belt from the arrow tree sculpture, with the ground three feet below me.

I stared at Psycho. 'What you doing?'

'Hanging you out to dry,' she said, then laughed and turned back towards the building.

'Where you going? You can't leave me here!'

But Psycho just raised a hand, in what might, or might not, have been a wave. All I could do was watch as she melted into the dark, leaving me alone with the faint aroma of coconut hanging in the air.

That was the word . . . coconut.

'Coconut,' I shouted after her. 'I meant, coconut!'

It's amazing how dangling from a ten foot arrow by your trousers can put a whole new perspective on things, G. I had plenty of time to replay the events that had led me there, and realized that once again I'd been a complete idiot. Psycho clearly didn't fancy me at all. Dad was an idiot too. No doubt I'd inherited my idiocy from him. But the most disturbing thing of all, was the fact that for a moment I had actually wanted Psycho Skinner to kiss me! I could blame it on the Bucks Fizz, but it didn't change the fact.

The need to empty my bladder was becoming urgent when I heard somebody calling my name and saw a figure silhouetted in the distant light from the gallery. The Space Hopper profile told me it was Meg. I shouted and waved, but it still took her ages to spot me.

'You take stupidity to a whole new level,' she said. 'Do you know that?'

'Any chance you could skip the witty banter and just get me down. I really need the toilet.'

'How did you get up there in the first place?' said Meg, reaching up and giving my legs a tug.

'Don't just pull!' I yelped. 'I've got things trapped up here!'

'Well, what do you suggest, Einstein?'

'I don't know, can't you unhook me at the back?'

Meg fumbled around behind me for a moment, but she's not as tall as Psycho and there was the bump to consider. After a few minutes of grunting and swearing she frowned up at me. 'You have tried undoing your belt, I assume?'

'You seriously think I've been up here all this time and not tried undoing my belt!'

'Yes.'

I tutted. Why hadn't I thought of just undoing my belt, G?

Because you take stupidity to a whole new level, Uncle Oz?

Shut up!

I undid my belt and fell face first onto the grass, narrowly missing my sister who swore loudly then kicked me.

There wasn't time to get back to the toilets in the building, so I relieved myself behind the arrow tree.

'How did you know I was out here anyway?' I asked as we walked back across the grass.

'The Tin-foil Tart said you were outside and needed me. I thought you were out here throwing up. I take it she was involved in you becoming a piece of living sculpture. What did you say to her? Something nasty I hope.'

I winced. 'It's . . . a long story. Somewhere around chapter twenty-four of an even longer story.'

Meg frowned.

'You'll have to read the book,' I told her.

I don't want to talk about the journey home, G. Suffice to say, Psycho acted as though nothing had happened. It was the combination of Bucks Fizz and Dad's driving that did for me in the end. Which is why I spent the following afternoon hosing down the back of the van and cringing as memories of the previous evening's events flooded back with unflinching clarity.

TWENTY-FIVE

'YOU CAN'T GO STRAIGHT FROM THE BEATLES TO DEAD FRANK'

Christmas turned out to be more of an out-of-date selection box than a new laptop and D-tags kind of deal, but at least I wasn't at school. There were a number of obvious reasons to dread the morning I would have to climb back into my battle scarred blazer. Every time Mum mentioned her exhibition—which she did at least five times a day—I'd taste orange juice and feel my stomach lurch. I knew I would have to face Psycho sooner or later—and later was fine by me. At least with the exhibition under way there had been no reason for her to come round during the holiday.

Then there was Ryan. I hadn't seen or heard from him since delivering my musical peace offering. I could only assume that he'd dumped the envelope straight in the bin the moment he saw who it was from. Though, the way things had been going, G, it wouldn't have surprised me to discover that my gift had managed to cause Ryan further pain in some way. Maybe the memory stick had contained a virus and wiped his computer, or Cyclops Dog at full volume had given Grandalf a heart-attack.

So I was surprised on the first day back at school when Ryan got on the bus and sat next to me. His face looked almost normal, with just the merest traces of yellow bruising under the eyes.

'I got your package,' he said, then frowned. 'Do you actually like that stuff? Or did you send it because you were mad at me for punching you?'

'What? Of course I like it!'

Ryan shrugged. 'That . . . what was it? Dead Fast Milkman? What was that all about?'

'Dead Frank's Supersonic Milkfloat,' I corrected him. 'Did you listen in the right order? Like I wrote down.'

He nodded. 'Well . . . I started with the first one, but I didn't get all the way to the end. Then I tried number two, but that wasn't much better. So I jumped to the last one—just to see what that was like.'

'Noooo!' I shook my head. 'No wonder you didn't like it. You have to build up slowly. You can't go straight from the Beatles to Dead Frank! That's like expecting a baby to play football the day after he starts walking.'

Ryan peered at me through his fringe. 'If you say so.'

'I do! You've got to listen all the way through—in the right order.'

'To be honest, Oz, I didn't really like them.'

'You have to give it time. You can't expect to like it straight away.'

'Why not? I liked the Beatles straight away.'

'Yeah, but that's because they're . . .'

'Good?' said Ryan.

'No! Obvious. Safe. Easy. The really good stuff you have to work for.'

'Why?'

'Because . . . ' I sighed, exasperated. 'You just do.'

'Oh.' Ryan picked at the clasp on his watch strap. 'Why did you post it through the door and run off like that?'

'I didn't think you'd take it, if you knew it was from me.'

'I wouldn't have taken it if I'd known what was on there!' he laughed, then his face went serious. 'It was Grandad's idea.'

'What?'

'Giving you a thump.' He shook his head. 'He's always going on about that's how they sorted everything out *when he were a lad*. Give someone a thump and he'll respect you. He forgets I'm not like him.'

'It doesn't matter. I probably deserved it.' I sighed. 'Look, I'm sorry about your nose. I don't know what happened, everyone was pushing and then you hit me and . . . it was like my arm just shot out.'

'It's OK. I started it.'

'Yeah, but . . . all that Kung-Fu Panda stuff.'

'That!' Ryan shrugged. 'They'll get bored and forget about it . . . eventually.'

We both grinned and for a horrible moment I thought he was actually going to hug me. Then his eyes widened. 'Hey! What d'you get for Christmas? Grandad bought me the *Time Gate Trilogy* on CD!'

'The what?'

'You mean you've never read *Traveller at the Gates of Time*!'

'Can't say I have . . . no.'

'What about *Prophet in the Land of Azgahrill*?'

'Is that the one where three blokes go on a fishing trip in the mountains, eat some bad mushrooms and end up in a flying saucer?'

Ryan frowned. 'You just made that up, didn't you?'

I grinned.

He shook his head. 'You've got to read *Traveller* at least. It's like . . . incredible!' I couldn't help but smile. I'd forgotten what Ryan was like when he got excited about something. He couldn't keep still and kept waving his hands around while he talked. 'I'll lend it you. I'll bring it in tomorrow. You'll love it!'

'I don't know. I'm not much of a reader,' I said. But Ryan wasn't listening.

I only saw Psycho once, from a distance. I'd been bracing myself all day for the moment when the details of my stunning Bucks Fizz fuelled performance would become public knowledge, but it never happened.

By my standards, G, it had been a spectacularly successful day. For a moment I even allowed myself to think that maybe this new year would be the start of better things.

Then I laughed.

TWENTY-SIX

THE IMPORTANCE OF BEING GONZO

'Where's the printer?'

'I'm using it.' Meg was sitting on her bedroom floor slicing sheets of paper with a Stanley knife, while the printer chugged away in the background.

'I need it. For homework.'

'You can have it when I'm finished.'

'You'd better not use up all the ink! What you doing anyway?' I knelt down and picked up the top sheet from a pile of fliers. There was a cartoon on the front showing a woman spitting out a mouthful of coffee and the words *Say NO to COFFEE-GO!* 'So now you don't want people to drink coffee?'

'We want people to boycott the Coffee-Go! drinks machines at college, until the principal agrees to change the supplier,' said Meg, not bothering to look up.

'Why? Don't you like their coffee?'

'It's not about their coffee, Oz!' Meg snapped. 'If you read the flier!'

'I can't be bothered to read all that! Neither will anyone else. There's too much writing.'

'Thankfully, *most people* can actually read, Oz.'

'Ouch! Was that a joke? Should I laugh now?'

Meg didn't answer.

'How many more of these are you going to print? I bet you use up all the ink!' I was about to leave when I spotted the photo on Meg's dressing table. 'Hey! Is this that ultra-scan picture of Gonzo? Dad said you had one.' I picked it up.

'Ultra*sound*!' said Meg. 'Put it down!'

To be honest, G, I was a bit disappointed. It was like one of those photos taken from space that people on telly get all excited about. They reckon it shows some distant galaxy, but all you can see is grey swirls and white dots. I was about to put it down, when suddenly my eyes adjusted and I could see you, clear as anything.

'It's an alien!' I said, staring at the huge transparent head and large black eyes.

'Moron!' muttered Meg.

'Look at that head—it's glowing. And the eyes!'

'That's the ultrasound, idiot! That's what they look like.'

'Are you sure? I mean, it could be like that film . . . the one where the alien bursts out of that bloke's stomach!'

'Goodbye, Oz!'

'I'm serious. What if you're incubating a whole alien race in there? I mean, do you really know where Kris is from?'

'I'm warning you, Oz!'

'Have you ever thought why he spells his name like that? Maybe that's what they do on his planet. That was his one mistake, the thing that gave him away!'

Meg grabbed a screwed-up ball of paper and threw it at me. I ducked and it flew harmlessly over my head onto the landing. When she snatched the Stanley knife from the floor though, it was my cue to exit.

'Hurry up with the printer!' I said, as I backed onto the landing and she slammed the door.

By the way, I was only joking about the alien, G. You looked like a dude.

A dude with a huge transparent head and boggly black eyes, but still cool.

The ball of paper Meg had thrown at me was sitting at the top of the stairs. When I picked it up and smoothed out the sheet, I saw it contained two columns of names. At first I thought it must be something to do with Meg's Coffee-Go! boycott, then I saw that some of the entries had *Osbourne* written after them, and I realized she'd been trying out baby names!

Aled—seriously?

Benedict—as if!

Clark—great, if you want to be called Superman your entire life.

Nye—what?

Marlon—was she joking?

I was almost impressed by the fact she had managed to maintain such consistently poor quality for the entire page. But you were in serious trouble, G. Intervention was required if I was to save you from a name that would bring nothing but grief for the rest of your life. Take it from your Uncle Oz—aka *Kecks*—names are important.

I took the list up to my room and crossed out each name Meg had written, then at the top of the page, in thick capital letters, wrote: GONZO. On my way back downstairs I folded the piece of paper and shoved it under Meg's bedroom door.

TWENTY-SEVEN

'YOU SHOULD NEVER KICK A PIG'

It was Elvin's first job of the day to see to the pigs. His uncle loved those pigs more than his family—more than his nephew, that was for sure. In the valley of Islatae, pigs carried more value than gold.

Elvin walked across the field towards the squat stone building that housed the beasts. The bucket of pig feed banged against his leg and the wind carried their richly pungent scent towards him.

I'd been reading for half an hour, and I was still only on the third page. There were five hundred and twenty-seven in total. At three pages every half an hour—six pages an hour—five hundred and twenty-seven divided by six . . . I found the calculator on my phone . . . eighty-seven point eight-three recurring. That's how many hours it would take to finish *A Traveller at the Gates of Time*. Three point six days of my life that I would never get back.

Ryan said he'd read the book eight times and I believed him. The edges of the cover were scuffed, and the pages themselves well-thumbed. Eight times! That was twenty-eight days! Ryan had spent nearly a month of his life reading this book, and I couldn't get past the third page. I sighed and shifted my position on the bed, screwing my eyes shut, then snapping them open again.

Elvin hated the pigs. They represented all that was wrong with his life. There was a whole world beyond the Cloud Mountains, a world of adventure and excitement, a world Elvin would never see. Sometimes he sneaked down to the tavern in the village to sit quietly in a dark corner and listen to the stories told by the travellers . . .

It would have been a lot easier to concentrate without all the shouting coming from downstairs. It was the familiar sound of Meg and Mum enjoying some quality time together.

Apart from the two mornings each week that Mum taught at the college, with her exhibition in place, she now had time on her hands. And with both hands restored to full working order, she was keen to put them to good use. We all knew she thought Meg had made a big mistake in deciding to keep the baby, but as always, Mum had decided to make the best of an unfortunate situation, which is how my sister's pregnancy became her new project. But it was doomed from the start. Mum and Meg are just too alike, and they both think they know best.

Mealtimes in particular had become a battleground, but weekends were the worst. With no college to escape to, and fewer shifts at the pub suddenly, Meg found it harder to avoid Mum's attention. The battle currently raging downstairs was one of the worst yet.

I put my fingers in my ears and turned back to the page.

Sometimes he sneaked down to the tavern in the village . . .

I was sure I'd already read that bit—

. . . to sit quietly in a dark corner and listen to the stories told by the travellers taking a break from adventure in the safe, green valley of Islatae. He listened to tales of distant planets, wars fought between armies of creatures unlike any Elvin had ever seen, or was ever likely to—except these pigs. He kicked out and one of the stinking creatures squealed in protest.

'You should never kick a pig.' The voice made Elvin start, and his eyes darted around the barn for a clue as to the speaker's identity.

Finally, some action! This would be the mysterious stranger come to take him off on the adventure he's been moaning about for the last three pages.

Elvin's eyes detected movement as a tall figure in a black travelling cloak and worn leather boots stepped from the shadows.

Told you!

Two floors below the voices were getting louder, and I was sure I'd just heard a crash. I put the book down. Elvis, or whatever his name was, would have to wait a little longer for his adventure. I needed to check on the real life drama going on in the kitchen.

I crept down to the landing and sat at the top of the stairs, from where I could hear without being observed.

'It was your decision to keep this baby, Megan,' Mum was saying. 'And I've supported you in your choice, even though I don't . . . '

'I know you don't want me to have it!' Meg cut in.

'It's not a case of that—'

'Well, what is it then?' I could tell Meg was getting fired up.

'If you'll let me finish.'

'Please do!'

I winced, picturing the balls of flame flying from Meg's eyes as she spoke. It was like a *Mega-Titans Clash* in *SlamShowdown*.

'Having a baby is a life changing event, Megan,' said Mum, blocking the fireballs with a wall of ice. 'You can't expect to just carry on the way you did before. You're going to have to make sacrifices—we all are.'

Meg snorted—sending a carpet of flame across the room. 'Well, I'm sorry if having a grandchild is going to be inconvenient for you!' she said, and Mum's icy defences dissolved in a hiss of steam.

'Now come on, Megan, that's unfair!' Mum turned the steam into hail, and sent it hurtling back like frozen marbles.

But my sister was ready. 'Is it? I mean, I wouldn't want my baby to get in the way of your work or anything.'

'What's that supposed to mean?' Mum had dropped her guard, left herself exposed.

'We've hardly seen you since we moved here. You spend more time in that barn with Wonder Girl from next door, than with your own family! And now, when it suits you—you swan back in here and start trying to take over my life!' I winced as Meg's firestorm engulfed our mother. That was an attack you didn't walk away from.

Or so I thought . . .

'How *dare* you!' Mum must have had an extra life saved up somewhere, not to mention a power boost. She sounded stronger than ever and mad as hell.

Sensing the new danger, Meg beat a hasty retreat. She moved so fast, I was still sitting at the top of the stairs when she barrelled past me into her room. Mum appeared moments later, but stopped when she saw me.

I grinned sheepishly and waved. Mum opened her mouth to say something, then shook her head and walked back into the kitchen. A moment later I heard the back door slam.

With the afternoon's entertainment over, I had no option but to return to the safe green valley of Islatae. Or maybe I'd just have a nap. It was a close call as to which would be the most exciting.

TWENTY-EIGHT

THE LIFE-SUCKING BRICK OF NONSENSE

I thought a week would be long enough to convince Ryan that I'd at least tried to read The Life-Sucking Brick of Nonsense. I'd finally made it to the end of the first chapter, where the tall dark stranger reveals to Elvin who he really is, and tells him that his destiny awaits beyond the Cloud Mountains. All of which, as you will testify, G, I predicted back on page three.

'You read it!' Ryan looked delighted. 'What did you think? Brilliant isn't it!'

I shrugged. 'It was OK.'

'I'll bring book two in for you tomorrow. That's even better!'

'No!' It came out louder than I intended. 'Thanks and everything, but I didn't quite read all of it, so there's probably not much point.'

'You didn't.' His face clouded. 'How far did you get?'

'Um . . . I read the first bit.'

'The first bit? Did you get to the *Council of Elders*? *The Fiery Gorge*?'

'I read the stuff about the pigs and the bloke in the cloak.'

'Wolffrun?' Ryan frowned. 'But that's right at the start—the first chapter.'

'I'm not much of a reader.' I felt bad, he looked so disappointed.

'It takes a while to get going. You need to keep reading. Once they reach the mountains it starts getting really good.' Ryan held out the book. 'Keep it until you've finished. You'll enjoy it, honest.'

'I'd better not—it'll take me ages. At least eighty-seven hours! Do you know how many days that is?'

Ryan gave me a funny look, then his face brightened. 'I know! I got it on audio book for Christmas! You can borrow that if you like. It's read by the author himself!'

'Really?' It didn't surprise me that the publisher couldn't find anybody else willing to read it, even if they *were* getting paid, but I didn't mention that to Ryan. Instead I heard my voice say: 'Yeah, OK. Great. Thanks.'

At least I'd got rid of The Life-Sucking Brick of Nonsense without hurting his feelings. I would now have to endure hours of some idiot reading me the pig boy's adventures, but I could cope with that. So long as I listened to the end, I could talk about it to Ryan, and he'd never know I'd missed out the rest of the book entirely.

We'd been back at school for nearly two weeks and nobody had mentioned the night at the Sculpture Park—which meant Psycho hadn't told anyone. Whenever our paths crossed, she acted like I wasn't there. I couldn't have asked for a better outcome. I should have been happy, except that the moment Psycho removed herself from my actual life, she started barging uninvited into my subconscious while I slept.

In my dreams, I finally found out what it was like to kiss the girl in the mercury dress—and learned that she tasted like chicken korma. More than once, after a particularly drawn out bout of kissing, Psycho stepped back and transformed into the praying mantis with the glowing red eyes. On each occasion I woke up sweating, my heart banging like a hostage trapped in the boot of a car. Afterwards I would lie awake trying to work out whether the most disturbing part of the dream had been when I was enjoying kissing her, or discovering I was about to be eaten.

The whole thing freaked me out so much, I had to tell Ryan—which meant divulging the entire Bucks Fizz episode in all its glory.

'You were drunk though, yeah?' he said, frowning.

'I suppose.'

'You drank three or four Bucks Fizz?'

'Could have been five. I lost count.'

'Did you eat anything?'

'No. Dad said there would be food there, but it was all rubbish little sausages and those mini flan things.' I pulled a face.

'You were drunk then, definitely. Your judgement would have been off. That's the only explanation. You're probably suffering post-traumatic stress disorder. Reliving the whole thing in your dreams. It's a common symptom.'

'So, you don't think . . . ' I paused, not sure if I could actually bring myself to say it out loud. 'It doesn't mean I fancy her or anything?'

'No chance! It's just your brain's way of coping with the trauma,' said Ryan. 'Trust me, you'll be fine.'

To some degree, Ryan was right. Compared to my first fun-packed months in Crawdale, nothing much happened for a while after that. Life slipped into a semi-comatose routine.

I went to school and Meg got fatter.

In between plumbing emergencies and jobs for the builder in Thackett, Dad finally got the central heating working, just in time for the warmer weather.

Meanwhile, I went to school and Meg got fatter.

Psycho started coming round to help Mum with a new set of sculptures, but we kept out of each other's way. Gareth hadn't bothered me since her intervention and although Ryan was still known as Frodopo, even that was beginning to fade.

I could feel my brain cells drying up through lack of excitement.

And all the time, Meg got fatter . . .

THE END

G MINUS 72

TWENTY-NINE

'IT'S LIKE YOU'VE GOT A WHOLE OTHER PERSON IN THERE'

The rain woke me up, rattling on the skylight like marbles in a bucket. I needed the toilet. By the time I'd gone down-stairs, my body had decided it was hungry. I remembered there was half a packet of HobNobs on top of the fridge—if Dad hadn't eaten them.

When I went into the kitchen, I found Meg sitting hunched on the back step with the door open. The hood was up on her coat, but she was still getting wet.

'Aren't you cold?' I said, sitting down next to her.

Meg shook her head. 'It's spring.'

'So I see.' I watched the rain hiss in waves across the yard, the guttering on the studio overflowing into the oil-drum barbecue like a waterfall. 'What you doing down here anyway? It's two in the morning!'

'Can't sleep,' said Meg, plucking something from a jar and crunching loudly.

'What's that?'

'Pickled gherkin. You want one?'

I pulled a face. 'I'll stick to HobNobs, thanks.'

Meg shrugged and blew her nose—which is when I noticed the notebook on her lap.

'Not making more lists of terrible baby names are you? I mean, seriously, Meg—who calls their kid Nye?'

'This from the boy who thinks I should call my baby Gonzo!'

'It's a great name!' I tapped the notebook. 'So what is it then? Don't tell me you're writing a book or something?'

'Notes for my Sociology essay on crime and deviance,' she said, flicking HobNob crumbs off the cover. 'Due in tomorrow.'

'Your *what* on *what*?'

Meg opened the book and read aloud. '*Examine the justifications for the right to commit crime in a modern consumer society.*'

I frowned. 'OK . . . some of the words I definitely recognized, but that's about it.'

She rolled her eyes and turned to face me. 'These days our society is all about consumption—owning stuff, yeah? The erosion of community and decline in family values reinforces the idea that we are all individuals and therefore free of obligations to others. This means, in a sense, there are no rules. You can do what you want, even commit a crime.'

'Says who?'

'Well . . . Doctor J. F. Silvester for a start. He did a load of research into the reasons people commit crime and wrote a book about it.' She reached down for another pickled gherkin. 'For instance, have you ever thought why we have laws?'

'Can't say it keeps me awake at night.'

'Exactly,' said Meg, crunching. 'Most people live their whole lives and never question anything. Governments rely on us being nice well-behaved citizens. OK, we might moan about the state of the country over a pint in the pub, but we don't actually *do* anything. People are either too lazy or too caught up in the latest reality TV show—which is just another sneaky trick the government uses to keep us distracted from what's really going on.'

'Hang on a minute. You're saying that *Star-Factor* and *Video Funnies* are actually part of an intricate government plot?'

'Could be!'

I snorted. 'Distracting us from what?'

'From everything! From the fact that your life is actually pretty rubbish. That the next person has got a better job, a bigger car, a wider TV! I mean, it's no coincidence that a tiny percentage of the population of most countries owns all the wealth. And guess what? They're also the ones running the country! What a surprise! So, the last thing they want is the rest of us going, *hang on a minute, I'd quite like a nice big car and a holiday home in the Caribbean too. Why should you lot have all the money and all the power? Why should I take any notice of your laws? They suit you, but they don't help me. I want that car, so I'm going to help myself.*'

'So that's what they teach you in Sixth Form college is it?' I said. 'Does Mum know?'

Meg sighed. 'One day, Oz, you might actually pull your head out of that bubble you live in and realize there's a whole world out there. Maybe then you'll . . .' She stopped and gave a sharp intake of breath.

'What?'

'I think the baby's woken up. He just kicked me in the ribs.' Meg rubbed the small airship concealed beneath her coat.

'That's Gonzo's way of telling you that you're talking rubbish!'

Meg tutted and undid some buttons, pulling her pyjama top up to reveal the blimp in all its glory. 'Watch!'

'What? You mean, you can actually . . . ' The words had barely left my mouth when I saw the skin on Meg's belly ripple.

'Whoa! That's freaky!'

'It's just the baby, idiot! If you give him a tap, sometimes he kicks back.' She gave the bump a gentle prod.

'Is there anybody in there?' I said, leaning closer. 'Kick once for yes, twice for no!'

'Quick!' she grabbed my hand and placed it on her belly, then yelped and pushed it off again. 'God, Oz! Your hands are freezing!'

'What do you expect? It's raining and the door's open!'

Meg pulled her top down. 'Now try.'

I rested my hand on the bump and gave it a tap. 'Hey, Gonzo! You in there?'

Now, I've been meaning to talk to you about this, G. You could have at least given me a little nudge. But no. Not a squeak. I sat there with my hand on my sister's belly for at least a minute and the only thing I felt was slightly uncomfortable.

'He must have gone back to sleep,' she said, pushing my hand away and pulling her coat closed.

A gust of wind blew the rain into our faces and I shivered. 'I'm getting soaked!'

'So go back to bed.'

But I stayed where I was, just listening to the rain and thinking about you, G—all curled up, warm and asleep right next to me.

'Did you know that at thirty weeks the baby's testes drop?' I said, remembering something I'd read in *Baby's Journey*. 'And at thirty-one weeks, he'll be going for a wee inside your belly! How gross is that?'

'You're obsessed, aren't you?'

I shrugged. 'It's interesting. Seriously—it's like you've got a whole other person in there!'

Meg raised her eyebrows and leaned back against the door frame. 'Most of the time I don't really think about it. I mean, I know I'm pregnant—I can't get away from that—what with the spots and the indigestion and needing to go to the toilet all the time.' She waved her hand over the small land mass protruding from the folds of her coat. 'And this thing weighs a ton. It feels like I'm carrying a bag of shopping strapped to my belly all the time. Oh, and everyone stares at me when I get on the bus, that's nice—and then there's Mum going on all the bloody time and . . . ' She stopped to take a breath and turned to me. 'What am I doing, Oz? I'm going to have a baby, for Christ's sake!'

'So you're not just getting fat then?'

'It's not funny!' She punched me on the arm. '*And* it's all your fault!'

'*My* fault! How d'you work that out?'

'Did you ever wonder why I couldn't go through with the termination?'

Of course I'd wondered, but I'd never quite found the right moment to ask.

'Before they would let me have it done,' Meg said, 'I had to sit down and talk to this woman counsellor—to make sure it was what I really wanted. But I was ready for that. I kept telling myself it wasn't a baby, just a bunch of cells. It didn't mean anything to me.' She pulled another tissue from her pocket and blew her nose.

'But you had to go and give it a name. You had to go and make him feel like a real person—calling him *Gonzo* and going on and on all the time.' She scowled. 'I was sitting there watching this woman's mouth moving, but all I could hear was your stupid voice: *Did you know Gonzo's as big as your thumb now? Did you know Gonzo's got hair?* And I knew it was too late. Thanks to you, the thing inside me was already Gonzo—already a person.

'So now I'm stuck with it. Stuck here in this bloody place, about to have a baby. And it's all *your* fault!'

I didn't know what to say. I felt quite proud to think that I had actually made a difference. That if it hadn't been for me, well . . .

Meg swore, then laughed. 'Tell you what. After I give birth, why don't I hand the baby over for you to look after?'

'OK.'

'You would too, wouldn't you? Christ, Oz! You haven't got a clue.'

'I know that Gonzo is over forty centimetres long and weighs approximately the same as a two kilogram bag of sugar.'

'Really? That's going to come in handy when he's screaming at four in the morning and you haven't had any sleep for days and you don't know why he's crying because you just fed him and he doesn't need changing. Yeah, that kind of knowledge is really going to help.'

I shrugged. 'I'd find out what to do. How hard can it be? He's just a baby.'

'Exactly! A baby! Jesus, what a mess!' Meg leaned forward and lowered her face into her hands. I listened to the soft pock of the rain landing on her hood, and noticed she was shaking. I wasn't sure if she was laughing or crying until she gave a big snotty sniff.

I felt like I should do something. So I reached out a hand and tentatively patted her on the back a few times. The crying stopped almost immediately.

Meg lifted her head and looked at me. 'What exactly do you think you're doing?'

'I . . . ' My hand was still resting on her back. I pulled it away and shrugged. 'I don't know . . . exactly.'

'Well don't,' said Meg. 'Ever. Again.'

'OK.'

'Now get lost and leave me in peace,' she said, digging in her pocket for another tissue.

I was tired by then anyway, and cold. My pyjama bottoms were completely soaked. I stood up. 'Well, night then.'

Meg nodded, but didn't say anything.

When I reached the door, I looked back and she was still sitting on the step, crunching on a pickled gherkin and watching the rain.

THIRTY

'WHEN DID YOU GET TO BE SO INTERESTING?'

'It'll be a laugh,' said Ryan.

'I don't know.' It was lunchtime and we were in the library. I was trying get some science homework done that was due in next lesson, but Ryan wouldn't stop talking.

'I bet you've never been camping, have you?' he said.

'What? No. Why would I want to go camping?'

'It's great fun. We have a bonfire and everything.'

I glanced up at the clock, then back at the incomplete worksheet on the desk.

'Seriously, Oz, you should come.' I'd noticed Ryan had started saying *seriously* a lot lately and wondered if I'd picked up any *northern* in return.

'Is your grandad going?'

'Yeah, 'course.'

'I thought he wanted to kill me.'

'He does . . . but he's always saying stuff like that. Anyway, he'll be too busy with the re-enactment to bother coming after you.'

'Re-enactment?'

'Yeah, it's *Fight Camp*, I told you!'

'Like that one you did before?' I remembered the photos on Ryan's wall and felt myself blush.

'Yeah, but this year we're doing the *Battle of Bucksnort Pass*, from *Traveller at the Gates of Time*! Have you got to that bit in the book yet?'

'I don't think so. They're stuck in the *Fiery Gorge* at the moment.'

'Hey, that's my favourite part,' said Ryan. 'When the—'

'Don't tell me!'

He grinned. 'Ha! I knew you'd like it! Told you it was good didn't I!'

'It's getting better. At least he's not still moaning about pigs!'

'Anyway,' said Ryan, 'we're camping in the woods in your village. You'd be mad not to come.'

I'll admit I was actually quite enjoying The Life-Sucking Brick of Nonsense, now I had someone else to read it to me. But that didn't mean I wanted to act it out—or go camping with a load of old people. I mean, what would Jack say if he ever found out? What would *anyone* say if they found out?

'Um . . . I don't know if I can.' I didn't have the heart to disappoint him straight away. I needed to stall until I could think of a good excuse. 'I'll have to ask my mum. When is it?'

'Next month,' said Ryan. 'Plenty of time to make the costumes and listen to the rest of the book.'

'Costumes?'

'Yeah, but don't worry. We've got loads of stuff you can borrow.'

I had a sudden vision of myself wearing a cloak and clutching a wooden sword. It didn't look good.

'By the way,' said Ryan pointing at my worksheet. '*Joules* has got an *o* in it.'

So has *social suicide*, I thought, as I corrected the answer.

Ryan was still going on about *Fight Camp* while we waited for the bus at the end of the day. The more excited he got, the louder he talked. I was relieved when he stopped suddenly and pointed across the road.

'Hey! Isn't that your dad?'

I looked up and saw the van pull into the kerb opposite. Dad was grinning at me through the open window.

'You two want a lift?' he shouted.

It was only when we crossed the road, that I realized Mum and Meg were sitting in the cab next to him.

'What's going on? Has something happened to Gonzo?'

'Gonzo's fine,' said Dad. 'I'm afraid you'll have to slum it in the back though, lads.'

Nobody was saying anything, but I guessed from the way Meg and Mum were sitting side-by-side, yet trying to keep as far away from each other as possible, that something had happened. I could also tell they weren't going to talk about it in front of Ryan.

'So what's going on?' I said, the moment he jumped out and closed the door.

Silence.

'Something must have happened or you three wouldn't be in the van together. It's Gonzo isn't it?'

'Oh, for Christ's sake!' said Meg, twisting in her seat. 'I got suspended from college, that's all!'

'*All!*' said Mum.

'Suspended! What for?'

'Does it matter, *what for*, Marcus?' Mum made it sound like it was my fault.

'I'm not ashamed,' said Meg.

'Well maybe you should be! Have you thought how this makes me look? I'm a member of college staff—and my own daughter gets suspended for criminal damage!' I hadn't seen Mum so angry for a long time. 'If you hadn't been pregnant, I doubt the principal would have been quite so lenient.'

'Criminal damage! What did you do?'

'I vandalized three drinks dispensing machines,' said Meg, unable to hide the pride in her voice.

'What?' Then I remembered the *SAY NO TO COFFEE-GO* fliers. 'I thought you were just going to stop people using them, not take them out completely!'

'I tried that, but I just got laughed at. It's like I told you—so long as they've got *Star-Factor* and a cheap cup of mocha-latté, people don't give a shit about anything else.'

'Megan!'

'It's true, Mum! I thought *you*, of all people, would understand!'

'I do understand. I just think there's a line and you crossed it.'

'I *tried* being polite. I wrote to the principal requesting a meeting and he refused. I asked people to show their support with a peaceful boycott and nobody would listen. Sometimes you've got to *cross* the line if you want to change anything!'

'Go Megan!' I said, leaning forward and slapping my sister on the shoulder. 'When did you get to be so interesting?'

'I don't see it's anything to applaud, Marcus,' said Mum. 'The only thing your sister has managed to achieve is to get herself thrown out of college and embarrass me at the same time. I don't see how that is helping anybody.' Mum had a knack for ruining the mood.

'At least everyone will be talking about it now,' said Meg. 'All the people who laughed at the fat girl handing out the fliers. Some of them might actually read what was on there now. Even if it makes one person stop and think, it'll be worth it.'

'That still doesn't change the fact that you've been suspended from college,' said Mum. 'I thought these A-levels were important to you.'

'They are, but I won't be taking them here anyway.'

Mum looked at her.

'I've been meaning to tell you,' said Meg. 'I'm moving back to Hardacre.'

THIRTY-ONE

WAY BEYOND THE CALL OF DUTY

I'd spent most of the afternoon in the attic, listening to The Life-Sucking Brick of Nonsense and thinking about Ryan's invitation to *Fight Camp*. Apart from the danger that someone might find out, there was the fundamental concept of camping itself, plus the whole *Grandalf wants to kill me* angle—which was a definite tick in the *against* column. Then there was the fact it would mean spending a whole weekend with the kind of people who thought it was perfectly reasonable to dress up and do play fighting in the woods.

Why was I even considering it?

Thinking always makes me hungry—something else I've inherited from Dad. I was on my way to sneak a crafty snack from the kitchen when I bumped into him on the landing. He was squeezed into his suit with the unreliable trousers again, and for a horrible moment I thought there was another family outing I'd forgotten about.

'What's going on? Why are you dressed like that?'

Dad raised his eyebrows. 'I'm guessing that what you meant to say was, *Hey, Dad! Looking sharp tonight!*'

I stared at him. 'If you say so. But why *are* you dressed like that?'

'I'm taking your mum out for our anniversary. You remember we gave each other cards at breakfast?'

I frowned at the vague recollection. 'Oh, yeah. I wondered what that was all about.'

Dad sighed. 'Well, I managed to get us a table at—' Then he stopped as we both heard the raised voices coming from downstairs.

Hostilities between Mum and Meg had increased since my sister's announcement of her plans to return to Hardacre and share a flat with Chloe. Mum and Dad were dead against it, and despite a week of sustained campaigning, Meg had so far failed to persuade them to change their minds. From the sound of things, she was still trying.

When we got downstairs, Mum and Meg were in the kitchen, facing off at either end of the table like two ping-pong players who had forgotten their bats. Mum had on the black dress from her exhibition opening, and Meg was still in her night clothes.

Since being suspended from college, my sister's appearance had deteriorated. She no longer bothered getting dressed and spent all day in the same tartan pyjamas and dressing gown, looking like an inflated Womble who had fallen on hard times.

'I'm sorry, Megan, but you're being extremely naïve about this,' Mum was saying. 'I'm sure it would be wonderful for the first few weeks—both of you looking after the baby together. But believe me, once the novelty wears off, and Chloe finds she can't get up for work in the morning because she's been kept up all night by a screaming baby, you might find it puts a different perspective on things.'

'Chloe isn't like that!' said Meg.

'Trust me, Megan. There will be times when even *you* will want to just walk away from that baby—let alone your friends. Don't underestimate how hard this is going to be.'

Meg was about to fire back an answer, when Dad intervened. 'Much as I hate to interrupt my two favourite girls, we really need to hit the road, love.'

Mum shot Meg a final icy glance, then turned away. 'I'll get my coat.'

'We'll probably be back late, so don't wait up!' said Dad. Then as he passed me on his way to the door, he whispered, 'Keep an eye on your sister, mate.'

I nodded. 'Have a good time. Oh . . . um, Happy Anniversary.'

'*Chapter Thirty-One: Escape from the Fiery Gorge,*' said the American voice in my ear.

I lay back on the bed, pretending not to notice the excitement buzzing in my gut as I waited for the next instalment of the pig boy's adventures. I couldn't believe I'd spent most of the day listening to it.

The smoke curled up from the gorge like grey fingers, wrapping itself around the travellers, stinging their eyes and filling their nostrils with the sour, putrid stench of sulphur. It was getting harder to see, and the rocky path was narrow and scattered with loose stones. Elvin knew that one wrong footstep would send him over the edge, plummeting into the abyss that was the Fiery Gorge.

There was a crash downstairs and the sound of breaking glass. I pulled the earphones out and sat up. Were Mum and Dad back already? I didn't think it was that late.

Another noise—like a chair falling over—then a thud.

What was going on down there? Was somebody trying to break in?

When I reached the landing Meg's door was open and her bedroom was empty. Not burglars then . . . unless Meg had heard them before me, gone down to investigate, and was now being held hostage with a hand over her mouth.

'Meg?' I shouted over the banister.

No answer. In fact, no sound at all—

Or maybe it was the sound of somebody being deliberately quiet.

I crept down the stairs, clutching my mobile, ready to dial Dad.

The kitchen light was on, so I pressed myself flat against the wall, like they do in films, and peered around the doorframe. I could see straight away that the window and the back door were still intact. The room itself looked empty.

'Meg?' I hissed. 'Where are you?'

I wondered if she was messing around, waiting on the other side of the door to jump out at me. I braced myself not to react, then stepped into the room.

My sister was lying on the floor by the sink, surrounded by broken glass. Her head was turned away and she didn't move when I called her name. When I saw the blood trickling down her wrist I thought she was dead.

For a moment I just stood there staring—too scared to move. Then her head slowly rotated towards me like a zombie re-awakening, and she grinned.

'Shit, Meg! You scared the life out of me!'

'Shhh!' she said, raising a bloody finger to her lips. 'I broke a glass. Don't tell Mum.'

'You're drunk!'

Meg giggled. 'You know what, little brother, I think I probably am. Would you care to join me?'

'What you doing on the floor?'

She shrugged. 'Just having a rest. I feel a bit sleepy.'

'You've cut yourself, look!'

Meg peered at the wrong hand. 'Have I?'

'The other one,' I said, feeling slightly light-headed at the sight of the blood dripping onto the tiles.

My sister tried to sit up. It was like watching a turtle trapped on its back.

'Hang on!' There was a large piece of glass on the floor next to her, with a red *VODKA* label still stuck to it. I kicked it out of the way, then threaded my arms under her armpits, but the moment I tried to lift, I knew it was hopeless. Meg was a dead weight, and then there was you, G—currently weighing in at over two kilograms!

Meg found the whole situation hilarious. 'You won't do it,' she said. 'I'm too fat. I'm like a big . . . fat . . . fish.'

'A fish?'

She nodded. 'A big . . . fat one. No!' Meg raised a finger. 'A big . . . fat . . . pregnant . . . fish!'

'I'm going to phone Dad.'

'No!' Her hand moved surprisingly fast, grabbing my arm. I felt her bloody fingers slip on my skin. 'Please!' She sounded desperate now. On the verge of tears.

'OK. But you're going to have to help me. Just watch out for the glass.'

'What glass?'

'On the floor.'

She looked around, then back at me. 'Did you break a glass?'

'No, you . . . look, just shuffle back, and don't put your hands down.'

It took a while, but with me pulling and Meg shuffling on her backside, we managed to get far enough away from the glass for Meg to get up, using me and the kitchen cupboards for support. Only now there seemed to be blood everywhere—smeared across the floor, the worktops and me.

My sister frowned. 'I need to wash my hands,' she said, holding her bloody palms out to show me. 'Dirty!'

I guided Meg towards the sink and turned on the cold tap. She'd barely put her hands under the water when her body twitched and she was sick all over the washing up. Some of the warm liquid splashed over my hands where I was supporting her, and I jumped out of the way. Unfortunately, Meg wasn't quite ready for standing unaided. She swayed, but I managed to grab her before the second eruption of vodka shot into the bowl.

And then she started to cry. Silently at first, then her whole body shook and I had to fight to keep her upright as she sobbed and retched and burped, cradling her face in her hands, while blood dripped off her elbow into the water.

'I'm sorry,' she said, after a while, in a voice that sounded more like her own.

'How much did you drink?'

She shrugged.

'Where did you get it, anyway?'

'Pub,' she said, through sticky lips. 'I stole it.'

'You stole it! You *stole* from Don Skinner!'

Meg nodded and spat into the sink. 'He deserved it—way he treated me! But I'm gonna get him, Oz.'

'What d'you mean?'

She turned her head and peered at me through matted hair. 'I'm going to rob the place,' she whispered, her eyes wide. 'Take all the money.'

'O . . . K.'

'I'm serious.' She coughed, retched and spat again. 'I'm telling you, he's a crook! You should see what goes on down there!'

'I know,' I said. 'Don't you remember? I tried to tell you the Skinners were dodgy, but everyone just took the mick!'

Meg shook her head. 'No! Don't take the *mick*! Take the money!' She laughed and burped. 'I'm going to do it!' she said. 'And then . . . do you know what I'm going to do then, little brother?'

I didn't answer, but I guessed what was coming.

'I'm going to get out of this place,' she said. 'Live with Chloe. And *they* won't be able to stop me.' Then she hiccupped and was sick again.

'Yeah, whatever you say, sis.'

If it hadn't been such a hassle. If there hadn't been quite so much sick and blood and broken glass everywhere, it would have been funny. At least I'd be able to tease Meg about this for . . . well, the rest of her life probably! The night she told me she was going to rob the village pub and run away!

When I was fairly sure Meg's stomach had nothing more to give, I helped her upstairs to the bathroom. The cut on her hand had finally stopped bleeding, but I couldn't find a plaster big enough to cover it. Luckily there was a roll of bandage in the cupboard above the basin. I wrapped that around her hand, until Meg looked like she was wearing one white boxing glove. Then I used a flannel to wipe most of the blood off her face. She still looked a mess, but it was the best I could do. Meg would have to sort out her blood soaked pyjamas and dressing gown in the morning.

'Thanks, Oz,' she said, her head wobbling as though it was too heavy for her neck. 'You're the best little brother in the world, d'you know that?'

'Yeah, whatever.'

I rolled my sister into bed, still wearing her boots and dressing gown—and left her to it.

Despite what Mum said, I had the feeling that my sister wasn't underestimating how much her life was going to change when she had a baby to look after. I think she knew exactly how hard it was going to be. That was the problem.

I stood in the kitchen and assessed the damage. The broken glass I could sweep up easily enough, but the blood smeared all over the worktops, the sink, and the cupboards looked as if it would take some scrubbing.

What if I left it for Mum and Dad to find when they got back? It wasn't my job to clean up Meg's mess. I'd already gone way beyond the call of duty. It wasn't my problem.

But I stayed where I was, staring at the smashed vodka bottle, the bloody handprints, the washing-up bowl full of sick. I imagined Mum and Dad walking in through the back door after their romantic evening and seeing it all.

I sighed and swore, then reached for the yellow rubber gloves under the sink.

THIRTY-TWO

SOMETHING STUPID

'Everything all right here last night? No dramas?' Dad slid two slices of toast onto my plate.

'Dramas? No.' I reached across the table for the peanut butter and avoided making eye-contact. I was glad Mum was still in the shower. It was no surprise Meg hadn't appeared yet.

Dad poured himself a mug of tea and stirred in some sugar, the spoon ticking like a clock. 'It's the weirdest thing,' he said, 'but I'd swear somebody cleaned the kitchen last night.'

'The kitchen?' I took a huge bite of toast and chewed slowly, buying time. 'Maybe it was Meg. You know . . . one of those pregnancy things.'

'*Pregnancy things*?' Dad looked at me.

I shrugged. 'We did it in biology. How pregnancy affects your hormones and can make people do weird stuff.'

'Right . . . So you wouldn't know anything about the blood-stained tea-towel in the bin then?' He was watching my face for a reaction, so I kept chewing while my heart raced around my chest like a headless chicken.

Then it occurred to me that once Meg finally got up, Mum and Dad couldn't fail to notice the bandage on her hand.

I sighed, 'I didn't want to say anything—but Meg broke a glass.' I looked at him. 'It was an accident, but she cut her hand cleaning it up.' I've learned that the closer a lie is to the truth, the more chance you have of getting away with it. Remember that, G.

'Cut her hand!' Dad looked worried. 'Is she all right?'

'She's fine. It bled a lot, but I bandaged it up for her.'

'It needed a bandage?'

'Not really, I just couldn't find a plaster. It looked worse than it was.'

Dad's brow creased. 'She just dropped a glass? It was an accident?'

'Yeah.'

'I'm worried about her, Oz,' he said, after a pause. 'She's been a bit low recently. I know she won't admit it, but getting suspended from college has hit her quite hard. And of course it's getting close to G-Day now . . . ' He gave a rueful smile. 'It wouldn't surprise me if she was terrified, the poor girl.'

I nodded. 'Probably.'

'But it was just an accident?' said Dad, again. 'She didn't . . . ' he was obviously struggling to put what was on his mind into words . . . 'do anything stupid.'

For a moment I wondered if I should tell him the truth. It had occurred to me that Meg must have been feeling fairly desperate to get drunk like that.

'Of course she did something stupid!' I said. 'This *is* Meg we're talking about, right? I mean, how hard is it to carry a glass from the cupboard to the sink without dropping it?' I forced my features into a grin and hoped it looked convincing from where Dad was sitting.

He laughed and took a bite from his toast, relaxing visibly. 'Thanks, mate! Sounds like you did a good job last night, looking after your sister. I appreciate it.' He reached across the table and gave my shoulder a squeeze, and for some reason I felt like a rat.

I was in my room staring at my French homework and listening to Dead Frank, when Meg appeared in the doorway. She'd changed her bloody pyjamas, but was still wearing the dressing gown and boxing glove bandage from the night before. Even by her own recent low standards she looked rough.

'Did you do this?' Meg held out her mummified hand.

'I couldn't find a plaster big enough.'

She came into the room and sat down on my bed. 'Um . . . what happened last night?'

'You don't remember?'

Meg shook her head. Close to, her skin looked grey and I could see her eyes were bloodshot. 'The last thing I remember was being in my room, watching a DVD. Then I woke up this morning covered in blood . . . and I had this.' She waved her hand.

'You don't remember the party?'

'Party?' Meg looked alarmed.

'Yeah, you and a bottle of vodka. I found you passed out on the kitchen floor. Blood and glass everywhere!'

She winced.

'Then you puked in the sink and told me you were going to rob the pub!' I laughed and Meg's eyes grew huge.

'Do Mum and Dad know?'

'Don't panic. I cleaned up for you. All the blood and the glass and the puke. Took me half the night. I'd only just gone to bed when they got back.'

Meg stared at me. 'You did that?'

'Which means you owe me—big time!'

She nodded.

'There is one thing, though . . . Dad found a bloody tea-towel in the bin. So I had to tell him you dropped a glass and cut your hand clearing it up.'

'In the bin? Oz! Why didn't you put it outside?'

'I put all the glass and stuff in the yard bin, I just forgot about the tea-towel—it was late!'

'What did Dad say?'

'He wanted to know if you'd flipped out, but I said it was just an accident.'

'He said that?'

'Not in those words, but that's what he meant.'

'You didn't tell him I was drinking?'

'Look, despite what you think, I'm not a complete moron.'

Meg gnawed the side of her thumbnail. 'I can't believe I got drunk. What an idiot!'

'Will Gonzo be all right?'

She glanced up at me. 'He's been kicking—complaining, probably—that's got to be a good sign, hasn't it? And if I was sick—that must have got rid of most of it. I mean, it can't have done any real damage . . . ' It sounded like Meg was trying to convince herself as much as me.

'So why *did* you get drunk?'

'I didn't mean to.' She sighed. 'I was fed up. I saw the bottle and thought *what the hell! I'll just have one to numb the pain.*'

I snorted. 'Just hold on while I get my violin!'

Meg's eyes flashed. 'You just don't get it do you?'

I shrugged.

'This place,' said Meg. 'It's driving me mental!'

'Huh! You and me both, sis . . .'

'You don't understand, Oz. *You* can go to school. One day *you'll* be able to leave. I'm going to be stuck here for the next God knows how many years. On my own—with a baby!'

'You won't be on your own. You'll have Mum and Dad . . . and me. We'll help with Gonzo.'

'That's the problem, Oz! Mum and Dad are doing my head in! I need to get away. Go and live with Chloe. I know it won't be easy, but it won't be easy here either. It's the only way!'

'What about me? If you leave, I won't get to see Gonzo!'

'You can come and visit. In school holidays and stuff. And I'll come up here sometimes . . . once Mum and Dad have calmed down.'

'That could take ages!'

Meg laughed through her nose and gave a weary smile. 'I'm sorry, Oz, but there's no other way. I'll go crazy if I stay here.'

'I can believe that! Some of the stuff you came out with last night!' I shook my head. 'Seriously! I wish I'd recorded it.'

'At least I didn't end up hanging off a sculpture by my trousers,' said Meg.

'At least I didn't end up ranting about robbing the village pub!' I told her.

She shrugged. 'But I am.'

'What?'

'Going to rob the pub.'

I stared at her. 'You were drunk! You were joking!'

'Was I?' Meg's eyes were steady, unblinking.

'You can't!' I laughed.

'Why not? Go on—give me three reasons why I can't do it.'

'Well . . . for a start it's illegal. It's not like stealing a bottle of vodka, or vandalizing a drinks machine. They'd put you in prison if you got caught—which, by the way, you clearly would. Two: how can *you* rob a pub? You need . . . equipment and stuff. And three . . . I don't know, you just can't. You don't need a third reason, one and two are good enough!'

Meg moved closer to me. 'Number one,' she said, her voice quiet. 'I know it's illegal, but I won't get caught. Don Skinner's a crook. He probably won't even report it. He doesn't want the police sniffing around down there.'

'But . . . '

She held up a hand. 'Number two. I do know how to rob a pub, or rather, I know how to rob *that* pub. And d'you know what the best part is?'

I shook my head.

'Nobody will ever suspect it was me, because everybody thinks like you. *How would a pregnant seventeen-year-old girl rob a pub?* Who's going to believe that? No one. Which is why my plan is so brilliant!'

I was waiting for Meg to smile. To laugh and point, and say something like—*ha! I got you going there didn't I? You actually believed I was serious for a minute, go on admit it!*

I waited, but it never happened.

'I've got a number three,' I said, 'and his name's Don Skinner! It's *his* pub, in case you've forgotten. He lives there. He's probably got guards and a big gun under his pillow. You're right, you won't need to worry about the police, because you'll already be dead!'

Meg snorted. 'Grow up, Oz! Skinner's a crook, but he's hardly *The Godfather*! He's just a mean, bigoted old man who deserves a taste of his own medicine for a change.'

'So, what are you going to do? Take it when you're next on shift? Won't that be a bit obvious?'

'There won't be a next shift. I got sacked.'

'What?'

'Let's just say Don didn't appreciate the way I served dinner to one of his sleazy mates.' A wry smile crept across my sister's lips. 'Beef and Ale Pie, straight in the lap. You should have heard him scream!'

'You tipped the whole dinner into his lap?'

Meg grinned. 'He deserved it. Making comments all night. The usual xenophobic, misogynist crap . . . '

'And I suppose you just *had* to put him right?'

'I couldn't just ignore it, Oz! The man was an idiot!' Meg shook her head. 'Of course he just laughed at me, and then started going on about me being pregnant and . . . other stuff. It was disgusting, and all Don did was laugh. So I *accidentally* dropped his dinner in his lap.'

'Go, Meg!'

She frowned. 'Don wasn't so impressed. I must admit, for a minute, I did think he was actually going to kill me. I've never seen anyone so angry. Then he called me a stupid girl. STUPID! GIRL! He said I was going to have to pay for the meal and the dry cleaning out of my wages. So I told him where to stick his job. Then he refused to pay up for the shifts he owed me, so I swiped the vodka for compensation. I didn't take it to drink. It was just there so I grabbed it.'

'But don't you think he'll suspect? I mean, you've got a motive.'

'Ha! I come way down the list of people with grievances against Don Skinner. Anyway, he's so arrogant, he wouldn't imagine for a minute that *I'd* do something like that.'

I shook my head. 'First the drinks machines at college, then the village pub. Don't you think you might be taking this whole new life of crime a bit too seriously? Whatever happened to saving the planet?'

'Sometimes you've got to save yourself first, Oz.'

'You're serious, aren't you?'

'Oh, yes, little brother. Very.' She looked at me. 'You know what I'm going to say next, don't you?'

I nodded, but she said it anyway. Probably because she liked the way it sounded.

And after all the other occasions on which Meg had threatened to kill me, this time I was tempted to believe her.

Afterwards I began to think I should have told Dad the truth at breakfast. It was obvious Meg had finally lost the plot, and I was fairly sure that planning to rob the village pub would come under Dad's definition of *something stupid*.

THIRTY-THREE

'CAN YOU EVEN *DO* AN OWL NOISE?'

She was joking, right? Maybe she didn't even realize she was joking, maybe she *thought* she meant it? Or she was still drunk . . .

It wasn't as though this was the first thing Meg had done that suggested her grip on reality was slipping. Ever since she'd woken up to find that Kris had deserted her, my sister's behaviour had become increasingly erratic. What if getting drunk was just another sign? A warning that next time she might do something *really* stupid. Something like robbing the village pub.

I had to tell someone. But who?

Ryan would get all agitated and start waving his hands about, but what good would that do? Besides, I didn't want it all round school that my sister was either crazy or planning on becoming a criminal. If I told Dad, he'd go straight to Mum, and once Mum got involved, there was no telling what would happen.

There was something else too. It sounds weird, G, but I'd started to feel differently about Meg. I'd always teased her about being some kind of wannabe superhero, but recently she'd really done it. I don't mean running around in lycra and a cape, but she'd had the guts to stick her neck out and actually *do* something. You had to respect her for that. After the other night I felt like she trusted me, and if I told Dad it would have seemed like a betrayal. But if I did nothing, would that be letting her down even more?

So it was that Elvin came to a decision. In the end it was easily reached. Once he understood that the only other option was death, what choice did he have? The situation was desperate. The last of their meagre supplies was gone, and he knew that if they did not get Anomar to a healer soon, she would certainly die. Elvin was not about to let that happen.

'I must light the beacon,' he announced to the ragged, battle-weary band huddled in the cave, 'to signal Wolffrun that the time has come to mount the attack. It will draw the Nyctal away, and provide us with our only chance of escape.'

'But that will mean assailing the peak,' exclaimed Sark. 'It's suicide!'

'It is my destiny,' said Elvin, smiling nobly. 'I can think of no greater honour than to give my life to save yours . . . my friends.'

'At least let me accompany you,' cried Pyralis. 'I can fly, and my night vision will help to guide us.'

Elvin smiled and laid a hand on the Mothman's shoulder. 'Your wing is burned, old friend. You can no more fly, than I. No, this I must do alone.'

'I'll come with you Uncle Oz!'

All eyes turned to the small figure standing at the entrance to the cave. The small boy with blue hair smiled back at them.

Eh?

Sark drew the blaster from his belt, but Elvin placed a hand on the warrior's shoulder and walked towards the child. 'Who is this Uncle Oz you speak of, friend?'

What?

I opened my eyes and pulled the headphones out.

Finally, you're awake!

Gonzo?

No wonder you fell asleep, that story's rubbish.

It was OK until you barged in and spoilt it!

Sorry! I was only trying to help.

Help? How do you plan to do that, exactly?

If you're going to be a grump, I'll go.

No! Sorry, I just woke up. It's OK. You want to help. That's great, thanks. Help with what?

You were worried about my mum—that she might do something stupid. I can help—keep an eye on her for you. Though, I did quite like it when she was drunk. It was like having a wave machine on! I went surfing—it was awesome! I think that might have been what made her sick though. That wasn't so good. Anyway, I'm offering twenty-four-hour surveillance. She won't give me the slip, I guarantee it.

I laughed—then stopped—as I heard the *ping* of a cartoon light bulb above my head.

'Now *that*—' I said, 'is not a bad idea at all!'

Meg was in bed when I got back from school the next day. The trail of dirty cups and plates across the floor suggested she had been there a while.

'Smells like someone died in here,' I said, wrinkling my nose.

'So leave.'

'Don't be like that, I brought you a drink.' I handed over the glass of orange squash Mum had asked me to deliver. 'Mum said to remind you about the antenatal thing at seven.'

Meg pulled a face and groaned. 'Oh, what joy! Just when I thought my day couldn't get any better.'

'What is it anyway? This *anti natal* thing. Some sort of protest?'

Meg spluttered and spat orange all over the duvet. 'Now that *is* funny,' she said. 'I wish it was a protest. In fact, that's not a bad idea. Maybe I could start one. An anti antenatal campaign. Boycott the Birth Plan!' She started laughing again.

'I don't get it.'

'A-n-t-e,' she spelt out, 'not a-n-t-i. It means *before* . . . it's Latin probably. *Ante*natal—*before* birth. It's just some stupid classes Mum's making me go to. Five happy smiley *normal* couples, plus Mum and me—the seventeen-year-old single mother—the sad act who couldn't even keep her boyfriend so she has to bring her mum to the classes. You should have seen their faces when we walked in last week. It makes going to the dentist seem like a fun night out.'

'What's it for though? I mean, what do you do there?'

'Apart from feel like a complete social leper?' Meg shrugged. 'It's supposed to *help us prepare for the wonderful day our baby arrives*—apparently. So far all they've done is scare the crap out of me with stories about how much it's going to hurt giving birth. It's a waste of time, but I haven't got the energy to argue with Mum about it.

'Hey, you should come,' she said. 'We could pretend you were my boyfriend—the baby's father. That would give them something to talk about! Go on, Oz. It'd be a laugh!'

'Nah, you're all right.' Since when was Meg such a prankster? 'Anyway, I need to talk to you.'

My sister raised her eyebrows when I closed the bedroom door.

'Are you still planning to rob the pub?'

She frowned and for a second I thought she was going to laugh and tell me not to be ridiculous. Then she nodded. 'There's a big party a week on Saturday—they'll be raking it in—more than enough to get me out of here.'

'So you're definitely going to do it then?'

'I just told you.'

'Well, in that case, I've been thinking,' I said. 'I could do with a new laptop, and *SlamShowdown Arena* comes out next month, so some extra cash would actually come in handy. I thought if you were going to help yourself, I might as well get in on the action.'

Meg scowled. 'Is this some feeble attempt at blackmail, Oz?'

'Blackmail? No! I'm offering to help—to do the robbery with you.'

'I thought you said it was a stupid idea? It couldn't be done.'

I shrugged. 'Like I said, I've been thinking. I changed my mind.'

'What makes you think I want any help?'

'Everyone knows you need a crew to do a proper heist.'

She laughed. 'I'm not robbing a casino in Las Vegas, Oz—this is the village pub.'

'So? It'll still be better with both of us. I could be the lookout. We can have a special signal in case I see somebody coming—make an owl noise or something.'

'Can you even *do* an owl noise?'

'Well . . . something else, then. Anyway, you are pregnant. I mean, what if something happened? You need someone to watch your back—and your front.' I grinned.

Meg studied me for a moment. 'Ten per cent.'

'What?'

'You can have ten per cent of whatever we get.'

'That's not fair! What's wrong with fifty-fifty?' I wasn't interested in the money, but if I didn't argue she'd be suspicious.

'Ten or I go alone.'

'Twenty.'

'Fifteen.'

I sighed. 'You've been working for Don Skinner too long! OK, fifteen.'

What did you do that for? I thought we wanted to stop her doing something stupid, not join in!

It was your idea!

I never said you should offer to help!

Yeah, but it was your idea to stay close and keep an eye on her.

Oh, I see.

At least now she won't do anything without telling me first. I'll get her to explain the plan. It's bound to be rubbish. Then I can talk her out of it.

Good luck with that!

Yeah, well—if she does go through with it, I'll just have to go with her. I can hardly let you two go blundering in there on your own, can I?

THIRTY-FOUR

'YOU'RE EITHER IN OR OUT'

'Did you ask your mum?' Ryan dumped his bag under the seat and slid in next to me.

'About what?'

He glanced around to check if anyone was listening. '*Fight Camp*.'

'Um . . . when did you say it was again?'

'A week on Saturday.'

I frowned. Why did that sound familiar? Maybe we *were* doing something that day and I wouldn't have to make up a reason why I couldn't go.

Then I remembered why *a week on Saturday* sounded so familiar. That would be the day I was helping my sister rob the village pub.

'I don't think I can,' I told Ryan. 'I'm doing something . . . with my family.'

His face fell. I could tell he didn't believe me. Maybe when he saw my picture plastered all over the local newspapers, underneath the headline *BROTHER AND SISTER GANG CAUGHT RED HANDED!* he'd understand.

Then I had a flash of pure Oz inspiration.

'Hang on—did you say *a week on Saturday*? Like, not this Saturday, but the one after?'

Ryan nodded.

'Oh, in that case I can come. I thought you said *this week*. Must be your accent!'

'Shut up!' said Ryan, but he was grinning. 'So, you *can* come? Definitely?'

'Yeah.'

'Brilliant!'

You may be wondering at my sudden change of heart, G, but it had just occurred to me that *Fight Camp* would provide the perfect alibi, should Meg decide to go ahead with the robbery.

'Hey, what you doing tomorrow?' said Ryan, as we got off the bus and trudged towards school.

'Dunno.'

'Come round to mine and we can start making the costumes.'

'Costumes?' I'd forgotten *Fight Camp* would involve dressing-up.

'There's a prize for the best one,' said Ryan.

'Yeah? What d'you win?'

'Last year it was a bottle of wine for the adults and book tokens for the kids.'

'Outstanding!' I don't think Ryan noticed the sarcasm in my voice.

'I won last year,' he said. 'I think it was the hobbit socks that did it.' Then he frowned and I wondered if he was thinking the same thing as me: was that book token worth all the grief those hobbit socks had caused him?

Fight Camp being held on exactly the same weekend as Meg was planning to rob the pub was too much of a coincidence to ignore. The Wheel of Destiny was on the move again, G, and now I could see where it was heading—on a direct collision course with the Beckett Arms pub.

'That's it?' I said. 'That's your plan.'

Meg scowled. 'What's wrong with it?'

What was wrong with it, was the fact that it was perfect. I'd been expecting some elaborate scheme requiring precision timing and an expert knowledge of explosives. Something I could pull apart, thus finally revealing to Meg quite how deluded she was. Instead I found myself thinking: this could actually work! In fact, I could see now why Meg was so keen to do it. Don Skinner was so arrogant, so sure that nobody would ever dare to try and rob him, he was virtually inviting someone to have a go. Which meant, the only thing I could say against it, was—

'It's boring!'

'It's simple,' said Meg. 'Which is why it's such a good plan.'

'Apart from one fundamental flaw,' I said.

'Which is?'

'We're going to be stealing from Don Skinner.'

My sister sighed. 'I didn't ask you to come along. If you're bottling out, I can do it on my own.'

'I'm not bottling out, I'm just saying.'

She frowned. 'Last chance, Oz. You're either in or out.'

I looked at her and gave a shrug. 'I'm in.'

THIRTY-FIVE

'I'VE NEVER BEEN A BAD GUY BEFORE'

The line of pictures across Ryan's duvet looked like a nerd identity parade. I began to wonder quite what I'd signed up for.

'Where d'you get those?'

'Off the internet mostly, fan sites and stuff. I drew a couple myself.' Ryan pointed to a black and white sketch that I recognized straight away as Elvin. He looked a lot more like Ryan than I'd imagined him from the descriptions in the book though. The other pictures were a mixture of very good, and shockingly bad, drawings of characters from the Life-Sucking Brick of Nonsense, plus a few photographs of people dressed up.

'These are all the characters Stefan said we still need,' said Ryan.

'Who?'

'He's one of the organizers. He makes sure we've got the right number of people on each side for the battle re-enactment.'

I scanned the row of images again and wondered if it was too late to run away.

'You can choose,' said Ryan.

Meg had been pleased with my idea of using *Fight Camp* as an alibi and had told me to pick a costume that would hide my face. 'How about one of those?'

'A Nyctal?' Ryan looked surprised. 'OK. Yeah. That could be really cool actually! I've never been a bad guy before.' He pulled a ring-binder from a shelf and started leafing through the pages. 'I think I've got instructions for making a Nyctal mask here somewhere.'

I knew from the book that the Nyctal were cyborgs—part human, part machine—but the picture made them look creepier than I'd imagined. Their faces, what you could see inside the shadowy cowl of their cloaks, were narrow and elongated, with glowing blue eyes and no mouth. The Nyctal fortress was the sulphur-filled Fiery Gorge, which probably explained why they were wearing gas masks. Except Ryan told me they weren't masks at all. He said the corrugated tube snaking down from what would have been the chin on a human was part of the cyborg's face.

While he talked, Ryan was pulling boxes out from under his bed, each one crammed full of clothing and bits of armour.

'There should be some cloaks in one of those,' he said. 'Have a look while I get the stuff for the masks.'

A few minutes later, he returned with two empty plastic milk bottles. I watched as he sliced away the back of one, then cut two eye holes either side of the handle, before turning it upside down and placing it over his face.

'How do I look?' His voice sounded muffled.

'Like somebody with a milk bottle on his face,' I said, but I was actually quite impressed. Especially when he put on one of the cloaks I'd found and pulled up the hood. It was amazing how an upside down plastic bottle could suddenly look like a cyborg head.

'I'm joking,' I told him. 'It looks just like the picture.'

Ryan took off the mask and grinned. 'You any good at papier mâché?'

Four hours later I was sitting on the floor of Ryan's bedroom picking dried glue off my fingers. Two Nyctal masks were drying on the windowsill, looking like excavated alien skulls.

'What are we going to use for the tube bits?' I asked.

Ryan pulled a coil of grey corrugated pipe from a bag. 'Old outlet hose from the washing machine. Grandad said he thought it might come in handy.'

The hose fitted perfectly onto the neck of the bottle.

'Bit of glue or gaffer tape should hold it,' said Ryan. 'If we cut it in half, it should do us both.' He grinned. 'You wait till we paint and weather them. We could win the best costume prize with these, you know.' He looked so happy, I couldn't help but grin back at him.

'Your sister seems a bit happier these days,' said Dad, as I helped him hang the Muppet wallpaper in the nursery.

I nodded, though I suspected that if Dad knew the reason for Meg's improved mood, he wouldn't be quite so pleased.

Despite the fact I'd agreed to do the robbery with her, and regardless of how possible it appeared, I had still been holding on to the idea that the whole plot was just Meg making a dramatic statement—like vandalizing the college drinks machines or dumping Beef and Ale Pie in someone's lap. I didn't believe my sister was serious, until she started getting dressed again and coming downstairs to eat with the rest of us. Being happy was what gave her away.

Once I realized, I knew I had to tell Dad, even if Meg hated me for it. Which is why I'd offered to help with the decorating.

'Here, slap some paste on that, matey!' Dad handed me the next strip of wallpaper.

I laid it on the pasting table, weighing down the corners to stop it rolling back on itself, and tried to work out how to break the news.

'Dad—can I talk to you about something?' I folded the pasted sheet and handed it back to him.

'I'm all ears, mate!' he said, climbing up the stepladder. 'Fire away, but grab the end of this while you're there.'

I helped him line up the pattern on the paper, rehearsing the words in my head.

Dad—you know how you asked me to tell you if Meg did anything stupid? Well, she's planning to rob the village pub tomorrow night.

'So, what's on your mind?' he said.

I swallowed and opened my mouth—but it was Meg's voice that rang across the room. 'Dad! Mum wants you in the studio.'

I turned round and saw my sister standing in the doorway watching me.

'Hold that thought, mate,' said Dad. 'I'll be back in a tick. Better not keep your mum waiting!'

When he had gone, Meg walked towards me, her arms folded on top of the bump. 'What are you doing?'

'Me?'

She rolled her eyes. 'There's nobody else here, Oz.'

I gestured around the room. 'Er . . . helping Dad wallpaper the nursery. What's it look like?'

'It looked like you were about to tell him something,' she said, her eyes fixed on me.

'Tell him something?'

Meg frowned. 'Do you realize how annoying it is when you answer by repeating the question?' She sighed. 'It sounded to me like you were about to tell him about tomorrow night.'

'Why would I do that?'

'I don't know.' She shrugged. 'Anyway, I wouldn't bother.'

'Because you'll kill me if I do, right?'

'Oh, no, nothing like that!' Her voice sounded suddenly bright and cheerful. 'It's just that I've changed my mind. You were right all along. It's a stupid idea. I don't know what I was thinking.' She laughed. 'So you're off the hook. Free to go and play in the woods with Brian.'

'His name's Ryan,' I said.

'Whatever.' Meg waved a hand dismissively and walked out of the room.

Now what was I supposed to think?

OK, she was probably lying—to stop me from telling Dad, or from going with her.

Either way, I realized that if I *did* say anything to Dad, Meg would just deny it. She'd laugh and tell him the whole thing was a joke—how she couldn't believe I actually fell for it. I knew which of us Dad would believe. It was like Meg said to begin with—who would suspect a pregnant seventeen-year-old girl? The fact that her plan was so preposterous, was exactly what made it possible.

THIRTY-SIX

A WEEK ON SATURDAY

At first glance, *Fight Camp* looked perfectly ordinary: different-sized coloured tents spread across a clearing in the forest, with two portable toilets at the farthest edge. Each cubicle had a sign sellotaped to the front: one was a drawing of Elvin, the other, Anomar—clues that all was not quite as it seemed.

As I watched, one of the doors opened. A man with a pot belly and a long blond wig stepped out. He picked up the large bow and quiver of arrows leaning against the portaloo.

'Is he supposed to be Elvin?'

Ryan looked up from the pile of green polyester and poles he was trying to assemble into a tent. 'That's Stefan. Him and his mates always get the best parts.'

'I thought Elvin was supposed to be young. He looks about fifty!'

Ryan grunted. 'Don't worry, we get to shoot at him tomorrow.' He grinned and sat back on his heels. 'Here, pass me those pegs.'

I handed him the bag and watched Stefan stroll through the camp, pausing to speak to Grandalf, who had his own tent further along the row. I was grateful we weren't sharing. The old man hadn't stopped scowling since Dad dropped me off.

On a patch of clear ground nearby, two young hobbits were engaged in a vicious game of Swingball, while a woman with pointed elf ears wandered around holding her mobile in the air trying to get a signal.

What was I doing here? Was it simply a convenient alibi for a robbery I wasn't even sure would go ahead? Or did I actually *want* to dress up and re-enact an imaginary battle from a fantasy science-fiction novel? Neither option seemed particularly likely, yet here I was.

Once the tent was up, Ryan took me on a tour of the camp. There was a second field, lower down the slope, steep and undulating.

'This is Bucksnort Pass,' said Ryan, 'or at least it is for the weekend.' He pointed towards the dense forest below us. 'Elvin's lot will attack from the south and we'll be up there.' We turned to look at the higher ground, covered in fallen trees and huge boulders. 'Should get a nice, well protected position—just pick them off as they come up the hill!' He laughed.

To be fair, *Fight Camp* lived up to its name—it was like some kind of secret combat training centre. I tried archery, with a real bow and arrow, and was shockingly bad, then managed to redeem myself during a paintball game in the woods. Our team won and when we were handing the equipment in at the end, the bloke asked if we wanted to sign up for the night game.

'How do you play paintball at night?' I wanted to know.

'With these.' He held up a packet of pale green balls. 'Glow-in-the-dark,' he said. 'You get a tactical flashlight too.'

'A what?'

'A torch,' whispered Ryan. 'What d'you reckon? Could be a laugh.'

I was about to say *yes*, when I remembered I was supposed to have a previous engagement. 'I don't know. I'm a bit . . . tired actually.' It sounded pathetic, even to me.

The man turned to Ryan. 'No reason you can't play, just cos your mate left his nuts at home!'

I could see Ryan was tempted, but he shook his head. 'Nah, I want to be fresh for the re-enactment.'

The paintball guy sighed. 'I'm disappointed, boys, very disappointed. I can't believe you're choosing re-enactment over the real thing.'

'The real thing!' said Ryan, as we walked away. 'Those Night Hunter guys are full of it. They make out like they're proper soldiers! All they do is run round trying to nick each other's flags!'

I suspected he was only saying it to make me feel better though.

Later in the afternoon there was a huge barbecue and everyone lazed around on the big field, eating and drinking. A few people tried to play football, but gave up after half an hour spent chasing the ball down the hill. I sat next to Ryan, on a large boulder still warm from the sun, washing a burger down with flat Coke. The roofs of some of the houses in the village were visible among the trees below, and at the very bottom of the hill, a faint smudge of white that was the Beckett Arms pub. The thought of what I had to do later passed like a cloud overhead, blotting out the sun and making me shiver.

When it got dark, Grandalf lit a bonfire and everyone sat round singing songs accompanied by a bloke on guitar and the woman with the elf ears playing a violin. My belly was comfortably full, and my body ached in that pleasant way that only comes from a day spent outdoors, doing stuff. It was past midnight when we finally crawled into our tent, but still a couple of hours before I would have to go down to the pub.

Ryan wanted to talk, but I needed him to be asleep before it was time for me to sneak out, so I yawned and mumbled and eventually he gave up. The only problem then, was staying awake myself. Tiredness acted like gravity, pulling me deeper into my sleeping bag. Meanwhile my brain argued that as Meg wasn't going to do the robbery anyway, I could go to sleep.

Except somebody wouldn't let me.

Hey! Uncle Oz! Wake up!

Why? It's fine. She said she'd changed her mind.

She was lying. She only said that to get rid of you. You've got to get down there!

OK. I'm going.

Don't go back to sleep.

I'm not. Stop nagging!

. . .

Uncle Oz! Wake up! You've got to go!

I jerked awake. What time was it?

Twenty to three—late already! I grabbed the cloak and my Nyctal mask, and at the last moment remembered the torch.

In the stillness of the sleeping campsite, unzipping the tent sounded like I was trying to start a motorbike.

'What you doing?' Ryan's voice was drowsy in the depths of his sleeping bag.

'Need the toilet. Go back to sleep.'

Outside, the cloudless sky was sprayed with stars. A low-slung gibbous moon coated the trees in silver. I shivered and wrapped the cloak around me, but it did little to dispel the bite in the air.

I picked my way between the tents, anxious not to wake anybody. Using *Fight Camp* as a convincing alibi relied on me leaving and returning unobserved. With any luck, Ryan would sleep through the whole thing and not realize how long I'd been gone.

The moment I stepped out of the clearing into the trees, darkness descended like a hood. The light from my torch just seemed to make everything outside the beam appear that much darker.

Being alone in a forest in the middle of the night is scary, G. It messes with your head. It doesn't matter how much you remind yourself that dark is just the absence of light, your brain is too busy dredging up all the scary films you've ever seen, all the stories of murderers and wild animals loose in the woods. When you're alone in the dark, the rules change.

The firm belief that I was being pursued by monsters got me to the edge of the forest in record time. I stood looking across the ash-coloured field to the Beckett Arms waiting at the bottom of the hill. I still didn't know if Meg would be there, but I had to check.

I kept to the shadows, hugging the hedges until I reached the cover of the large bushes bordering the car park at the rear of the pub. That was when I noticed the van—a white Transit with its back doors open, parked so it was facing the exit.

That's odd, I thought.

Then a figure emerged from the building.

Meg?

But the person was male, too tall and clearly not pregnant. He deposited a large crate into the back of the van. It seemed a strange time to be making a delivery, but then this *was* Don Skinner's place. The man turned to go back inside, and that's when I saw he was wearing a mask. It had holes for the mouth and eyes, the kind people wear to go skiing—

Or to commit a robbery.

Could he be working for Meg? Had she ditched me in favour of some bloke with a van and more experience? I felt a pang of some emotion I couldn't, or maybe didn't want to, put a name to.

I moved along the line of bushes, trying to get a better view.

Somebody else appeared—shorter and fatter, but still not my sister. This one also wore a ski mask and was dressed all in black, except for his trainers, which were white and seemed to glow in the moonlight. He loaded another two crates into the van and returned to the pub.

If the men were working for Don Skinner they wouldn't be wearing masks.

They *had* to be robbing the place.

I checked my watch and scanned the shadowy field for my sister. I was on time and at the rendezvous point we had arranged when I was still part of the plan, but there was no sign of her.

What if she *was* somehow involved with Ski Mask and Trainers? But Meg wouldn't be interested in stealing crates of booze. This was all wrong. I could feel it in my guts.

Maybe Meg had already been inside the pub when the men arrived. What if she was in there now? Hiding—or being held hostage.

Hang on!

Hadn't Meg told me the robbery was off? Just because I didn't believe her, didn't mean she wasn't telling the truth. There was a good chance that my sister was happily tucked up in bed while I crouched in the bushes having a heart-attack. In fact, the longer I stayed there, the more convinced I became that Meg was at home and I was an idiot. Strangely enough, G, that thought made me feel a lot better.

And then I heard the scream.

THIRTY-SEVEN

WORST CASE SCENARIO

The noise had come from inside the pub—or had I imagined it? Perhaps it was an owl. But it hadn't sounded like an owl. It had sounded like a girl.

I strained to listen in case it came again, but all I could hear was my own ragged breathing inside the stupid mask. I took it off and tried to think. No matter how much I didn't want to accept the fact, I knew it was Meg I'd heard scream. What other explanation could there be? She must have come down early, got inside the pub, then run into Ski Mask and Trainers.

Wasn't this exactly what I was supposed to be protecting her from?

But what could I do against two grown men? For all I knew there might be more of them inside—possibly armed.

I was going to have to get help.

It felt like running away, but my phone was back at the tent. If the police arrived and found Meg in a mask, with a crowbar hidden under her coat, it wouldn't look good, but what choice did I have? I had to do something—so I kept moving, hoping inspiration would strike by the time I got to the camp.

Going up hill was a lot harder and the track seemed to go on for ever. I began to wonder if I'd taken a wrong turn, and paused to sweep my torch across the trees looking for a landmark I recognized.

That was when the lights came on—blinding and surrounding me—and a disembodied voice barked from the darkness.

'Drop your weapon and put your hands in the air!'

I raised my arms as a figure clad in black stepped into the light. The body armour and helmet he was wearing made him look like a giant insect. It took me a moment to realize I'd stumbled into the Night Hunters.

'Look, I'm not part of the game,' I said, lowering my hands to shield my eyes against the light. 'I need to get back to camp.'

'Do you surrender?' he said.

'Yeah, whatever—look, I really haven't got time for this.' I tried to push past, but he blocked my path and pressed his gun into my chest.

'Come on, mate, you're supposed to stay in character,' said a voice behind me.

'I told you! I'm not in your stupid game!'

'It's a trick,' said someone else. 'Check him for weapons.'

'For Christ's sake! There are people robbing the pub in the village. We need to get help.'

'Robbing the pub?' Insect Man raised his visor. 'Is this a joke, lad?'

'No! It's not a game. It's not a joke. It's real! Real people! Robbing the real pub!'

'How do you know?'

'Because I saw them!' I shouted. 'They're wearing masks! Carrying stuff out of the pub and putting it into their van! What do you think they're doing? Moving house?'

And then everything happened really fast. There was a sharp crack, somebody yelped and the lights went out.

'Get down!' shouted Insect Man. 'We're under attack!'

Then another voice, strangely familiar, called my name from the darkness and told me to run.

So I did.

Once we were sure the Night Hunters weren't coming after us, we stopped running. Ryan lifted his mask and grinned at me. 'Did you see that? I shot him!'

'You *shot* him?'

He pulled a paintball gun from under his cloak and waggled it in the air. 'I borrowed this from Stefan's Land Rover. You don't want to be outside camp without one when there's a game on.'

'What are you doing here anyway?' I said, gulping for air.

'I came looking for you. Where did you go?'

I told him about the men robbing the pub.

'The Beckett?' said Ryan. 'Skinner's place!'

I nodded. 'Only . . . I think they've got my sister.'

'What?'

'It's complicated—I'll tell you later. We've got to call the police . . . or something!'

Ryan shook his head. 'There's no signal up here, but I've got my phone. Come on.' And he started running down the hill.

The white Transit was still parked outside the pub, but there was no sign of any people or any noises.

'Good, they're still here,' said Ryan.

'That's good?'

He turned to me and his face was serious. 'If they've got your sister, Oz, they might be using her as a hostage. We can't let them leave in case they take her with them.'

'What?'

'We need to keep them here until the police arrive.'

'Why would they take her with them?'

'Insurance—to make sure they get away.' He shrugged. 'It happens all the time. And the first rule of being a hostage is don't let them take you anywhere. If they do, you're as good as dead!' Ryan must have seen the look on my face, because he added. 'Not always—that's just worst case scenario—but there's no harm making sure they can't leave.'

Ryan put his hand on my shoulder and gave what I'm sure he thought was an encouraging smile, while I tried to decide if I was going to be sick or not.

Then he called the police from his mobile, but I could tell they didn't believe him. Ryan gave his name and address, but thankfully didn't mention me. Meanwhile, I tried to think of plausible reasons Meg would have for going to the pub at three in the morning, ready for when they arrived.

This was all my fault. I should have told Dad. I should have told Mum—ages ago. If I'd done the right thing, Meg would be at home right now, not being held hostage in a pub. Not about to be . . .

'Oz, are you OK?' Ryan was frowning at me.

I nodded.

'I'm going to let the tyres down on their van,' he said. 'That should slow them down a bit. You stay here and watch the door.'

'The door?'

'Yeah, in case they come out.'

'What am I supposed to do then?'

'Just start shooting. That should give me time to get away.'

I stared at him. 'Shooting?'

He handed me the paintball gun. 'You won't kill anybody, but a shot in the balls at close range should slow them down.' He laughed and lowered his mask, then before I could protest, disappeared through the bushes. I watched him crouch down next to the van, and after a few seconds, heard the hiss of air escaping from a tyre.

There hadn't been a sound from the pub since we arrived and no one had been in or out.

Come on, G—talk to me. What's going on in there?

No answer. Just the hiss of the tyre and Ryan's feet on the gravel.

My hands were shaking, but at least the sick feeling had subsided a little. I looked down at the paintball gun. Maybe I should go in there. I couldn't stand just waiting, doing nothing—not knowing if you and Meg were all right.

Then Trainers was in the doorway with a crate in his arms. He was halfway to the van before I remembered I was supposed to do something.

In my haste to fire, I pulled the shot wide, but the crack of the gun was enough to make him pause and glance in my direction. For a few seconds he was stationary and facing me. I couldn't miss. Five shots in quick succession, straight into the tender target area Ryan had suggested.

Trainers opened his mouth, but the cry of surprise and pain was drowned out by a series of rapid explosions as the bottles he'd been carrying hit the ground. He crumpled to his knees just as Ski Mask appeared behind him.

I fired again, but the shots burst harmlessly against the wall, dripping down the white brickwork as though the building itself were bleeding.

For a moment Ski Mask looked confused, afraid even—then he saw the paint splatters and let out a roar.

He ran towards me, shouting and swearing, promising all kinds of pain.

When he burst through the bushes, I turned and ran.

I could hear his breath, feel his feet thumping the grass, getting closer all the time. If I could just make it to the trees I might stand a chance.

When I glanced up to check how far I had to go, the shock of what I saw almost tripped me.

At first I thought the forest was on fire. Then the line of flaming torches emerged from the trees revealing an army of fantasy creatures. Elves and Nyctal, hobbits and Mothmen, wizards and goblins swept towards us down the slope waving an array of medieval and space-age weaponry above their heads. The chain of fire stretched the width of the field, and the air was filled with the pounding of feet and the roar of voices raised in battle cry.

Behind me Ski Mask skidded to a halt, swore, then turned and ran.

Elvin's army swept after him, flowing past me like a river, flooding the pub car park where Trainers was scrambling to his feet. He didn't stand a chance. I watched as the man went down under a scrum of Mothmen. Ski Mask made it to the van, but for some reason never started the engine. Within moments he was surrounded by a ring of flaming torches, guns and swords trained towards the cab.

And it was over.

By the time I got back down the hill there were already people inside the pub. A man dressed as Wolffrun stopped me before I reached the door.

'Better not,' he said. 'Don't want you disturbing the crime scene.'

I was about to argue when Don Skinner appeared, wearing the same silk dressing gown I'd seen before. He smiled and acknowledged the cheers and applause that greeted him, but I noticed his hands were shaking. Then I saw movement inside the building, as somebody else walked towards the exit.

I pushed past Wolffrun, then stopped—

Psycho Skinner stepped through the doorway with a coat around her shoulders.

Stefan was behind her. 'That's everyone,' he said.

I waited until I was safely in the shadows of the hedge before pulling off my mask. The cold air was a relief from the sweat pouring down my face.

'Hey! I wondered where you'd gone!' said Ryan, walking towards me. He grinned. 'We did it! We stopped them!'

'Yeah.'

'Where's your sister? Is she OK?'

I shook my head. 'It wasn't her. I heard a scream and I thought it was Meg, but it was Psycho!'

'Psycho?'

I nodded. 'She must have been helping out at the pub and slept over.'

Ryan stared at me. 'You mean we did all that to save Psycho Skinner?' He sat down on the grass and laughed until there were tears rolling down his cheeks. Then he wiped his face and looked up at me. 'I understand why Psycho was here. What I don't get is why you thought your sister would be.'

Before I could think how to answer, I heard the wail of a siren approaching, and saw red and blue lights flashing across the hillside.

I knelt down next to him. 'Listen! If you speak to the police, don't mention Meg or me.'

'What?'

'Tell them it was you—on your own. We're dressed the same. Nobody'll remember.'

'Why can't I tell them the truth?'

'It's complicated . . . I'll explain later, I promise. It's just better if no one knows I was here. I'll sneak back to camp. Pretend I slept through the whole thing. Please!'

Ryan stared at me, then he shrugged. 'If you want. Doesn't seem fair though. I mean, you were the one who stopped that bloke.'

'It doesn't matter,' I said, handing him the paintball gun. 'You told me to shoot him in the balls, so that's what I did. No big deal.'

No big deal.

All a mistake.

A misunderstanding.

Meg was never there.

Officially . . . neither was I.

THIRTY-EIGHT

'JUST KEEPING AN EYE ON EVERYTHING'

A few hours later I was sitting on the grass outside the tent eating a barbecued burger for breakfast. The sun was shining and the events of the early hours had taken on the quality of a half-remembered dream. After an exchange of stories—with participants giving their version of events to people who hadn't been there—the attention of the camp turned back to the big geek-off taking place that afternoon.

I was washing down my late breakfast with warm lemonade when Ryan pointed across the field and said, 'Isn't that your dad?'

Shielding my eyes with a hand, I looked and saw a familiar figure in khaki shorts picking his way between the tents. Something kicked in my chest.

I scrambled to my feet and jogged towards him. 'What are you doing here? What's wrong?'

'Morning, Oz. Good to see you too!'

'Dad! What's going on?'

'Everything's fine.' He placed a large hand on my shoulder—not a good sign. 'Megan fell down the stairs last night,' he said. 'She's all right, but . . . '

'Gonzo!'

'She went into labour.'

'What?'

'She had the baby, Oz. Last night . . . well, this morning actually.'

'She can't have! He's not due yet!'

'Lots of babies are born early. They've got a special unit at the hospital to look after them until they're strong enough to manage on their own.'

'So Gonzo's going to be OK?'

'They're both in good hands, mate.'

'What does that mean?' I didn't want to say it out loud, but I had to know. 'Gonzo won't die will he?'

'Our Gonzo? No way!' Dad put his arm around my shoulder and squeezed, but I wasn't convinced.

'I want to go and see them.'

Dad grinned. 'That's why I'm here.'

Mum was waiting for us in the hospital lobby. She didn't say anything, just hugged me.

'What's wrong?' I said, pulling away. 'What's happened to Gonzo?'

'The baby *and* your sister are both fine,' she said.

'Really?'

'Can we just take him up,' said Dad. 'He won't believe us until he sees them with his own eyes.'

We went up in a lift that smelt of bleach and then Mum led us through a set of double doors labelled *Neonatal Intensive Care Unit*, which didn't sound good.

I'd expected a ward with beds like you see in hospitals on TV, but Mum showed us into a room that looked more like a science laboratory. There were banks of machines everywhere, bleeping and flashing. It took me a moment to spot the large plastic boxes amongst all the equipment. Inside each one was a small wriggling thing, attached to the machines by wires and tubes.

Then I saw Meg, sitting on a chair in the far corner. She waved and smiled, but I could see it was an effort.

'Hey, little brother. You look like shit!'

'You too,' I said, and she grinned.

Then I looked in the plastic box next to Meg's chair and saw you, G. I couldn't believe how small you were—not much bigger than one of my trainers. And you were red, not blue—and I could see tiny veins like roads on a map all over your skin. There was a little white hat on your head and a clear plastic tube going up your nose. Your eyes were closed, but I could see your tiny chest moving, and it had all these wires stuck to it with little blue plasters and some strange red light thing attached to your foot.

'What's all that for?'

'They're just keeping an eye on everything,' said Mum. 'Just until the baby gets stronger.'

There was a screen above the box, with different coloured numbers flashing and those wavy lines like you see in hospital dramas—the ones that go flat to show someone's died. All of yours were jumping up and down though, G, like you were drawing a row of sharp teeth.

'So . . . what do you think?' said Meg.

I looked up and realized they were all watching me. 'Is he going to be OK?'

'The doctor said she'll need some help breathing for a few days,' said Meg. 'And they want to do more tests, but yeah, she should be OK.'

I nodded, then it registered what Meg had just told me. '*She*?' I stared at her, and noticed they were all struggling not to laugh. 'What?' I looked back at you, G—lying there all innocent, like it was nothing to do with you.

'But Gonzo's a boy!'

'Well, Gina is definitely a girl!' Mum moved next to me and put a hand on my shoulder. 'Isn't she beautiful!'

'That's what you're calling her then? Gina.'

'My mum's name was Georgina,' said Mum.

'You didn't really think I was going to call her Gonzo, did you, Oz?'

I didn't answer—just stared at you.

Gina, not Gonzo.

THIRTY-NINE

'TIME TO MAN-UP AND ACCEPT THE CONSEQUENCES'

Ryan was officially a hero. The *Crawdale Echo* had it plastered all over its front page: HERO SCHOOLBOY FOILS ROBBERY! There was a picture of Ryan outside the pub, wearing his Nyctal costume minus the mask. He was standing between Don and Psycho Skinner, while Stefan and a few of the other *Fight Camp* people crowded round trying to look menacing.

According to the article, Ryan had *noticed the men entering the pub and alerted camp leader, Stefan Tolkien-Smith, who quickly gathered a band of plucky volunteers to storm the pub and apprehend the gang, holding them until the police arrived*. It explained that *quick thinking* Ryan had stolen the keys from the gang's getaway vehicle and then been *forced to defend himself with a paintball gun*!

When I saw how much of a celebrity Ryan had become, I did wonder if I'd been hasty in my decision to remain anonymous, but I was happy for him. I hoped it might make up for everything he'd been forced to put up with because of me.

I should have guessed that not everybody would be so impressed.

'It wasn't me!' I stared at the moustache and glasses adorning Ryan's face on the newspaper article pinned to the school noticeboard. 'Honest!'

'I thought that were your trademark, Kecks!' said Gareth, slapping me too hard on the shoulder.

Ryan frowned at the picture.

'He probably did it,' I said, as Gareth sloped off laughing. 'If I'd drawn them at least they wouldn't be lopsided.'

'Doesn't matter,' said Ryan. 'You were right, moustaches are funny.' And then he took out his pen and drew one on Psycho.

'What are you doing?' I said, horrified. 'She'll think I did it!'

'Nah!' Ryan laughed. 'Isobel's all right. I'll tell her I did it for a joke.'

'Hang on! This is *Psycho* Skinner we're talking about, yeah?'

He frowned. 'I think we should probably stop calling her that. I mean, it's a bit childish. And she's actually all right, once you get to know her.'

I stared at him. '*Once you get to know her*! Since when were you two mates?'

'She came round to say thanks—brought me a card and a big box of chocolates.' Then he stopped and his face was suddenly serious. 'But, look—you don't need to worry. I'm not trying to muscle in or anything.'

'What are you talking about?'

'Me and Isobel, we're just mates. I don't fancy her or anything.'

'So?'

'So . . . you can ask her out, I don't mind.'

'What? Why would I want to ask her out?'

'You clearly fancy her.'

'Me?'

Ryan lowered his voice. 'I didn't realize at the time, but you knew she was in the pub didn't you. That's why you wanted to get help. And then there's all those dreams you keep having.'

'You said that was trauma!'

He laughed. 'I was just trying to make you feel better! Maybe it's time to man-up and accept the consequences, Oz!'

Accept the consequences? Of all the outcomes of drawing that moustache on Psycho Skinner's picture, I'd never imagined this as one of them. Ryan was deluded. Fame had clearly affected his judgement. So why did my chest tighten when we stepped into the quad and I saw Isobel walking towards us?

'Hey, Isobel! We were just talking about you,' said Ryan.

She frowned.

'Yeah, Oz was wondering if you'd like to go out with him some time?'

I'm not sure who was most surprised—me or Isobel.

'Is that supposed to be funny?' she said, glaring at me.

'No!' I croaked.

'*You* want to go out with *me*?' Hearing her say it like that, proved how ridiculous it was. But there wasn't a safe answer to the question. Which is why I said—

'If you want.'

Isobel stared at me and I could see her face was having difficulty finding an appropriate expression. Eventually she snorted. 'I'd rather go out with a rotting corpse,' she said, then shook her head and stalked away.

I turned to Ryan. 'What did you do that for?'

'At least now you know where you stand.'

'And that's supposed to make me feel better is it?'

He laughed. 'Anyway, I bet you don't have any more of those dreams now.'

He was wrong about that too.

The *Neonatal Intensive Care Unit* at Thackett Hospital was only a short distance from Crawdale High, so rather than getting the bus home after school, I walked across town to see how you were getting on, G.

After two days in the room with all the machines, you'd been moved down the corridor to somewhere called the *Low Dependency Unit*. You were still inside your plastic box, but there were fewer tubes and wires. The nurses said you were getting better at breathing and eating, so Meg was allowed to wrap you in a blanket and hold you for a while.

Usually when I arrived, I'd find either Mum or Dad already there, but on Friday it was just you and Meg. It was the first chance I'd had to talk to her about what really happened that night.

'Were you ever seriously going to rob the pub?' I asked.

For an instant Meg looked alarmed and glanced around the room, then she grinned. 'Of course I was.'

'So you were on your way to the village when you fell down the stairs?'

Meg smiled and raised her eyebrows. 'Ah, now that would be telling.'

'Oh, come on! What difference does it make now?'

Just then you made a noise and squirmed. We both looked at you.

'I didn't have a chance,' said Meg. 'This one decided she wanted out!'

'What d'you mean?'

'I got a contraction. That's why I slipped. It was her.'

'So, if she hadn't . . . you'd have gone down to the pub?'

'Maybe, who knows?' Meg grinned. 'I still reckon it would have worked. The plan was perfect—simple, but perfect.'

'Except somebody else got there first,' I reminded her.

'Yeah! Imagine if we'd gone down there too—all of us fighting over who was going to rob it!' She laughed. 'And then your little mate coming down and being a hero! I can't believe you slept through the whole thing!'

I shrugged. 'So you're not planning on running off to Hardacre for a while then?'

Meg shook her head. 'To be honest, Oz, I'm too tired to do anything.'

FORTY

G

I could hear you crying from the end of the yard. That noise was becoming the soundtrack to our lives. Nobody was getting much sleep now you were home, G.

Meg was in the kitchen, walking around in agitated circles, while you howled into her face. I knew babies cried, but this firestorm was something else. The weird thing was that there never seemed to be any particular reason why you should be so angry. Often you just woke up and kicked-off the moment your eyes opened.

'Sounds like somebody's awake then,' said Mum, following me in from the studio with her goggles still perched on her head. She washed her hands, then walked across to Meg.

'What's all that noise for, lady?' she said, holding out her hands to take you.

Meg hesitated, then passed you over and I waited to see if it would happen again.

Sure enough, the moment Mum lowered you onto her chest, the hundred decibel howling quietened to a whimper. Your big black eyes surveyed the room for a moment and then you leaned your head on Mum's shoulder and yawned. It happened every time, like magic—as if Mum knew the location of some hidden mute button. You could tell it really annoyed my sister.

'I just fed her, so she'll probably be sick,' said Meg.

'You're not going to be sick are you, beautiful.' Mum stroked your head and your eyelids began to droop. 'By the way, what time's Kris arriving?' she said, turning to Meg. 'If you want to go and have a bath, I'll have Gina for a while.'

'It's no big deal, Mum. He's coming to see the baby, not me.'

'I know. I just thought you might like a rest.'

'I *can* cope you know!'

'I'm not suggesting you *can't*! I'd just like to spend half an hour with my granddaughter.'

'I thought you were working?'

'I can take a break.'

It's always like this. Mum tries to help and Meg thinks she's interfering—which she is sometimes, but not always. On this occasion Meg relented. She muttered a thanks and stomped off upstairs.

A few minutes later Dad walked in carrying a bulging rubbish sack with off-cuts of Muppets wallpaper poking out. 'Madame's room is prepared,' he said, pausing to waggle your foot as he passed. It was like he'd pulled the puke lever. You burped and sent a stream of white liquid down Mum's front.

'Oops!' said Dad. 'I'll get a cloth.'

'I think I might need to change, actually,' said Mum, surveying the regurgitated milk trickling down her jeans. 'Oz, could you take her for a minute.' She held you towards me, but I hesitated. You were frowning again. A sure sign that things were about to get nasty.

'She doesn't like me. She'll scream. She always does.'

'Just for a minute, Oz, while I get cleaned up.'

'Don't let her see you're scared,' said Dad. 'Babies can smell fear!'

'I thought that was dogs,' I said, as Mum deposited you into my arms.

It still surprised me how light you were—like a toy.

As expected, the moment you looked up and saw me, your face screwed up into a fist of fury and you erupted. I held you against my chest, worried I'd drop you, the amount you were kicking and squirming. And the heat coming off you was incredible.

'Try walking with her,' said Mum. 'Just put her against your shoulder and walk around.'

'How's that going to help?' I shouted over the din, but I tried it anyway.

To my amazement, the maelstrom actually started to wane.

'I used to have to do that with you,' Dad said. 'First few months you barely slept. Every night about two o'clock you'd start screaming and wake the whole house up.' He shook his head. 'I'd have to take you out so your mum and Meg could get some sleep.'

I laughed.

'Wasn't so funny at the time,' he said, grinning. 'We were out for hours some nights. The moment I stopped moving, tried to sit down or look in a shop window, you'd start up again. I must have walked miles!'

It was hard to imagine that part of my life—doing things I have no memory of. I don't suppose you'll remember any of this, G, which is why I decided to write it all down. It started with that stupid letter at school, but for some reason I kept writing. I thought one day you'd be able to read it and find out what really happened while we were waiting for Gonzo.

And now you're here. A hot, snuffling, farting, puking, squirming thing on my shoulder. A real live person. Undeniable.

Except you're not Gonzo.

Just by being here, you prove that he never existed.

But he did—

Without Gonzo everything would be different.

Without him, you might not even be here.

And that's OK, G—because even though Gonzo's story might be over—

Yours is just beginning.

Abandoning childhood plans to be an astronaut, DAVE COUSINS went to art college in Bradford, joined a band and moved to London. He spent the next ten years touring and recording, and was nearly famous.

Dave's writing career began aged ten, penning lyrics for an imaginary pop group. He has been scribbling songs, poems and stories ever since. His debut novel for teenagers, *15 Days Without a Head* was a *Sunday Times* Children's Book of the Week, and a winner of the Society of Children's Book Writers and Illustrators *Undiscovered Voices*. A member of author collective The Edge, Dave spends his days at schools and libraries meeting readers, or at his desk in the attic making up stories. (Sadly, Albert, the anarchic cat mentioned at the back of *15 Days*, has since departed on an adventure and is yet to return home.)

Keep up to date with Dave (and Albert) at www.davecousins.net.

ACKNOWLEDGEMENTS

Writing a story is a solo activity. Turning that story into a book takes a huge collaborative effort. *Waiting for Gonzo* would never have emerged from the attic if it hadn't been for the belief and hard work of a team of talented people. Thanks and credit should go to:

The entire OUP family—Jasmine Richards and Claire Westwood for their editorial insight and belief in *Gonzo* from the start. Jennie, Hattie, and Helen, for looking after me on tour and for putting up with me on a weekly basis! Liz, Elaine, Charlotte, Lou, Anne-Marie and her team for their energy and advocacy; Kate for her eagle eyes at the copyedit stage; Jo and the design gang for their creativity and patience, plus all the crew out on the road, taking the books to the readers (with particular thanks to Karmjeet Kaur for being a tireless champion and posting press cuttings to me from far and wide).

In addition, the following folk were kind enough to give their time and share their expertise: Joanna Cannon checked my wounds; Caroline Graham-Males gave me an insight into the care of premature babies; Rhys Williams shared his knowledge of renovating ancient farmhouses on remote hillsides; and Viv Martin managed not to laugh at my attempts to write Latin and politely put me right. Special mention and massive thanks to Michael Fewtrell for bringing Dead Frank's music to life and making it possible for the rest of us to hear the contents of Oz's playlist (visit www.davecousins.net to listen to the tracks).

I would also like to take this opportunity to thank everyone who has supported me in my writing adventure so far. Readers—without you there would be no point in any of this! Friends, family and fellow writers—especially

the Society of Childre
and the authors at The E
co.uk) for their friendship a
all the bloggers and journalists
for spreading the word about *15 D*
Finally, a huge shout out to all the teach
booksellers, without whom books would ne
way to readers. Respect to you all for keeping g
current climate of financial hardships and short-s
government policies. (A special thanks to Tina and all the staff at my local Waterstones.) Sorry, I can't mention everyone by name, but if you're reading this, you probably know who you are!

Finally, my home team: Sarah Manson, still the best agent in the world, who is tireless in her enthusiasm and ridiculously generous with her time and wisdom. My friends for telling *their* friends about *15 Days* and for reminding me there is life outside the attic. My parents for sharing their love of books, and for their feedback during one long afternoon in a pub in Wakefield, when *Gonzo* was taking its first faltering steps. My 'outlaws' Ma 'n' Pa Raven, whose support and encouragement is way beyond the call of duty. Love and thanks to Ptol and Hock—always there in spirit and online!

Biggest thanks and much love to Jane and Dylan who gave honest opinions on each draft, pointing out the plot holes and bad spelling. They always believed that *Gonzo* would be worth the wait and were never afraid to tell me to shut up and get on with it.

Dave Cousins, 2012.

LOVED WAITING FOR GONZO?

HERE'S AN EXCLUSIVE PEEK AT DAVE COUSINS' FIRST NOVEL:

AVAILABLE NOW!

MEET LAURENCE, FIFTEEN YEARS OLD AND SIX FEET TALL. VERY SOON, HE'LL DRESS UP AS HIS MUM AND IMPERSONATE A DEAD MAN ON THE RADIO . . .

The skirt doesn't look too bad, but my hairy legs definitely spoil the effect. I turn away from the mirror and look through Mum's drawers for a pair of tights. I've never worn tights before and I put a massive tear in the first pair, trying to get them on. I'm more careful the second time and manage to get the tights onto my legs without any damage—except now, the crotch part is hanging just above my knees. After a lot of tugging and wriggling I pull them into the right position. It feels weird, but my legs do look a lot better.

Now for a top. Mum doesn't go much for flowery feminine clothes. She dresses like a man most of the time, but that's not going to help me look like a woman. The best thing I can find is a white blouse with tiny blue flowers. The buttons do up the wrong way, so it takes me a while to get it on. It doesn't look too bad . . . but there's still something not quite right. But what?

Then I see the lacy black bra on the floor by the bed. No way!

But if I want this to work . . .

It takes me an age to get the stupid thing on, because

it does up at the back. In the end I take it off, fasten it and then pull it on over my head. It has to be the most uncomfortable thing I've ever worn. The lace itches and the straps cut into my shoulders. I don't know how Mum does it. I stuff the bra with the ripped tights and some socks, then check the effect. It looks like I'm trying to smuggle potatoes down my top. I need something less lumpy.

The only thing I can find is a huge jar of lavender bath salts that must have belonged to Nanna. I fill two socks with them, fold over the ends and slip them into the bra cups. The effect is actually quite realistic, except one is noticeably larger than the other. I even them out and try again. It'll have to do. I smell quite . . . flowery as well now, which can't be a bad thing.

I take Mum's black puffa jacket from the cupboard and put that on. It might look a bit odd in this weather, but it puts another layer between the public and my bath-salt boobs. I try to squeeze my feet into Mum's long boots, but they're miles too small. I'll have to make do with trainers. I get the feeling people won't be looking at my feet anyway.

I check the final effect in the mirror. It's definitely better with the sunglasses on. They're huge and hide most of my face. Luckily, I don't really have to shave yet and with the wig and the sunglasses, plus a good smear of Vampire's Kiss, I almost look like a woman. But will almost be enough?

It has to be. All we had to eat yesterday was one Mars bar each. It feels like someone is sticking knives into my gut and it's swollen up like a balloon. At least I'll have Jay with me—that will make it look more believable. Most people give Jay all their attention anyway, they probably won't even notice me.

FURTHER INFORMATION

Waiting for Gonzo is a work of fiction, but many young people encounter problems similar to those faced by the characters in the story. The organizations below are available to offer confidential advice to anybody seeking help for themselves, friends, or family members.

The helpline telephone numbers listed here are for the UK, but there will almost certainly be similar support services in other countries. Your school or local library may also be able to provide information on help available.

If you discover that you are pregnant, there are several organizations that can offer help, advice, and support. Even if you are under 16, you can seek confidential advice from your doctor, local family planning clinic, or by calling **NHS Direct** on 0845 4647.

If you are under 25, you can visit a **Brook Centre** for free confidential advice. To find your nearest centre, go to www.brook.org.uk or www.askbrook.org.uk.
Helpline: 0808 802 1234 (Calls are free from all phones including mobiles) Text: AskBrook on 07717 989023 (standard SMS rates apply).

The Family Planning Association offers advice on pregnancy, contraception, abortion, and sexually transmitted infections.
Website: www.fpa.org.uk Helpline: 0845 122 8690 or 0845 122 8687 in Northern Ireland.

The National Childbirth Trust is a UK charity dedicated to supporting parents of all ages, providing impartial information and introductions to local support networks.
Website: www.nct.org.uk Helpline: 0300 330 0700
Email: enquiries@nct.org.uk.

F COU

Marie Stopes International offer information and advice including unplanned pregnancy counselling.
Website: www.mariestopes.org.uk/Are_You_Late
Helpline: 0845 300 8090.

ChildLine
www.childline.org.uk offers advice on a wide range of issues facing young people.
You can call ChildLine at any time on 0800 1111. Calls are free and confidential.

Bullying UK offers help and advice to young people, parents, and schools on how to deal with bullying.
Website: www.bullying.co.uk Helpline: 0808 800 2222.

One in every nine babies in the UK is born either ill or premature, with one being admitted to special care every six minutes. **Bliss** is a UK charity working to provide the best possible care and support for all premature and sick babies and their families.
Website: www.bliss.org.uk Telephone: 0500 618140
Email: hello@Bliss.org.uk.

A Word of Warning
Please exercise caution when using the internet. If you receive bullying or inappropriate messages, images, or other material while online, don't hesitate to report it. The following websites contain helpful information regarding online safety and what to do if you experience any problems: www.thinkuknow.co.uk, www.kidscape.org.uk, www.childnet-int.org/report.